EDDY DECO'S
LAST CAPER

EDDY DECO'S LAST CAPER

An Illustrated Mystery

◀ **by** ▶

Gahan Wilson

𝕿imes BOOKS

Library of Congress Cataloging-in-Publication Data

Wilson, Gahan.
Eddy Deco's last caper.
I. Title.
PS3573.I4569538E3   1987   813'.54   87-40194
ISBN 0-8129-1671-9

BOOK LAYOUT BY QUINN HALL

Manufactured in the United States of America

9   8   7   6   5   4   3   2

FIRST EDITION

To All of Us
Trying to Be
the Good Guys

EDDY DECO'S
LAST CAPER

CHAPTER

◄ 1 ►

It's a little joke of mine to call the place where I have my office the Rundown Building, but that's not to say it didn't have dreams once; you can easily tell it did from the winged stone lady on its front.

Day or night, rain or shine, she blows her horn in bas relief over the main entrance, and she and the frieze running over and under the first- and second-story windows show that the builders meant well, show they really cared; but the builders built in the wrong part of town and the fine, successful people they'd hoped for never came to rent their offices and look good in their lobby, just the bad ones, the lost ones, and so over the years the Rundown Building's been holding the wrong party and that's soured it and turned it bitter in all its parts.

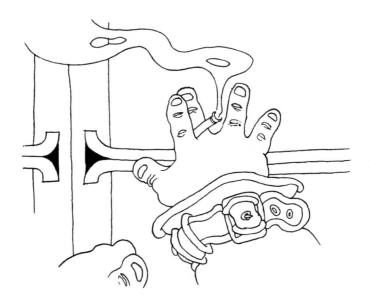

The elevator, for instance, would like to go in any direction but up or down, so it's always fighting the walls of its long cage, always gnashing its cables, and sometimes when you signal for it, deep in the small hours of the night when everybody's gone but you and there are only shadows in the offices and hallways, it won't come, and you know it's out of sheer perverseness. You can hear the buzzing in its cabin stories down when you push the button, but it just squats there at the bottom of its tunnel, all lit up for nobody, and refuses to budge. Sometime I guess it'll try to trap me between floors one night when it's feeling particularly nasty, and that'll be a story, but I know in broad daylight with witnesses around it'll never try a trick like that because it hasn't got the guts.

The corridors try to cheer things up, all that pretty marble in all those pretty patterns, but they don't make you smile like they may have once because they've all been broken and badly fixed too many times like an old boxer's face, and nobody's been thoughtful enough to give them the kind of cleaning they've really wanted for years.

The door leading to my inner office is tucked around the corner from the client's entrance so I can get in and out with nobody the wiser if that's my mood, which it oftentimes is and was today seeing as how it had been a rough night, what with one thing and another.

I'd run into too many mean people and drunk too many bad drinks and it all still hurt a little, and when something woke me up far too early this morning, a woman crying in another apart-

ment or sad, loud music coming from a radio across the street, or maybe the two of them ganging up on me together, I couldn't get back to sleep because even though Arnie Parker was dead, since I'd finally managed to kill him, what Arnie had done to my shoulder still ached too much to let me do it, so I'd taken a little of the whiskey I leave on the bedside table for just that sort of emergency and now I took a little of the whiskey I keep in a drawer of my desk for the same.

I guess it would be more than fair to say I was just as happy to have a few moments to myself to try and relax a little and see if I could glue myself back together, but none of it worked because I found staring at the morning's paper only served to bring back memories I could just as soon do without.

I buzzed for Verna.

It's painful to admit it but you could say Verna hates my guts, what with this and that which has happened over the years between us, things we'd both like to forget—Verna in particular, I'm sorry to say—but can't. I don't hold any of it against Verna, that's my way, but she just can't seem to get past it.

"A lady is waiting to see you, and something else," Verna said.

"I think I can make time for the lady," I said. "But I'm afraid the thing puts me a little too much in mind of the coastline around Red Hook in Brooklyn. Nothing personal, you understand, just bad associations."

"What's the lady's name?" I asked.

"Tracy McEstings. She told me her father is Colonel Esterhazy. She said you knew him. She said everybody knew him."

"Tracy, eh?" I said. "That would make her the old man's youngest daughter. She looks a lot like her sister, from what I see. I missed meeting her that time the Colonel hired me when some unfortunate hobbies of his oldest daughter had gotten her involved with a group of people who were asking for more money than the Colonel wanted to give them. My understanding was that Tracy was in Europe getting into other kinds of trouble the Colonel didn't care to speak of."

But Verna didn't want to talk about the lady; she wanted to talk about the thing.

"It's been here a long time before the lady," she said in that tone of voice she sometimes gets, the one that irritates me and makes me want to go somewhere else. "Ever since midnight in the hallway outside. It's kind of cute once you get to know it. I think it's lonely."

I smiled at Verna the way I can and told her to explain to the thing that the lady had a long-standing appointment and to usher in Tracy McEstings, and then I ignored her until she did it.

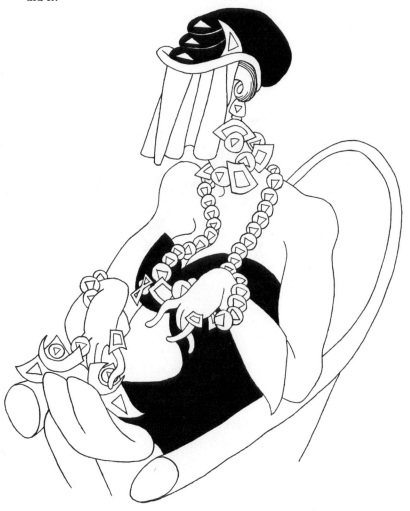

It would be less than honest to pretend that Tracy Mc-Estings's silhouette had only partially prepared me for her effect on me in the flesh. She was wearing black velvet and diamonds, mostly diamonds, including one pinful of them for each breast, and of course they both deserved it. Nothing concealed much of anything except a veil she had around her face.

"Are you in mourning?" I asked.

"You might say I'm practicing," she said in a husky voice that went well with everything else.

"From the thought you've given to your costume you seem to be looking forward to the actual event," I said, but she was too busy getting a cigarette together to listen to me.

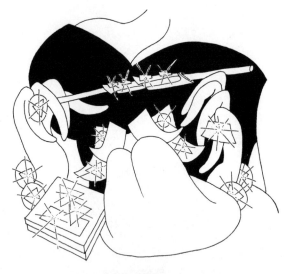

Before she could get out her diamond lighter—I assumed it would turn out to be a diamond lighter—I did the job for her with the simple stainless-steel one I carry for myself. It got a funny little dent in its front stopping a bullet Greasy Joe Golick meant for my heart, but it still lights up a lady's smoke if you're firm with it.

"Thanks," she said, and I really liked the way her throat moved when she said it.

"It's part of the service," I said. "But you didn't come up here just for that. My experience with daughters of Colonel Esterhazy is that they require more in the way of help from private detectives than lighting up their cigarettes."

Once again she wasn't listening to me on account of getting things out of her purse and I hoped it wouldn't become an established habit. Finally she worked her way down to what she'd been looking for and held it up like a trophy.

"Who's sending you notes from Chinatown?" I asked.

She started and took a long look at the top of the slip of paper. Apparently she'd never noticed the return address before.

"Say," she said, "you really *are* sharp!"

I wasn't all that surprised at her reaction, as I'd had some experience with her older sister, so I just went on: "And what do they mean by 'this'?"

"I suppose it's rhetorical," she said.

"I think you're misusing 'rhetorical,'" I said, "but forget that, put that to one side—did the note come attached to something?"

She went through the business with her purse again and came up with something that gave me that funny little feeling

you sometimes get in this business that lets you know you're about to see something disgusting.

"Have you looked inside?" I asked.

"No," she said. "I just never thought of that."

"Don't feel bad about it," I said. "If people like you could think, people like myself wouldn't ever get work. What do you say we both have a look, now that we've thought of it?"

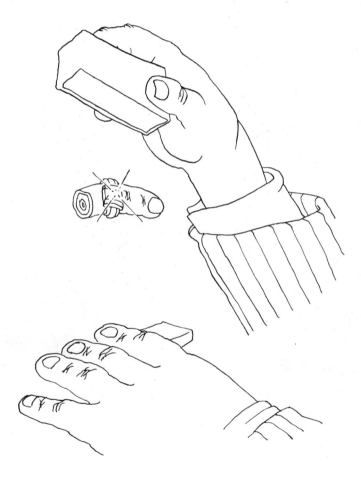

"More diamonds," I said. "Do you know that finger, Mrs. McEstings?"

"I ought to," she said. "It's my husband's."

Then, because she had fainted, I rang for Verna even though I could see she was busy.

"Take care of Mrs. McEstings, here," I said.

"What's wrong with her?" Verna asked, nudging her with

one toe in a way that showed pretty clearly she didn't care all that much for our client.

"She's a little dim, like her sister," I said, "and not much help on a case, so I'm going to see their father."

CHAPTER

2

The Esterhazys bought the land this town sits on from the Indians and they still own most of the important parts. They built their family mansion with an eye to impress and it still does even if people build lots bigger buildings, nowadays. Besides, the chances are that Colonel Esterhazy or one of his corporations either owned all the skyscrapers in sight or that they sat on land rented from him.

Scheme, the butler, and I were old pals from the last time I'd worked for the Colonel. I'd want a butler just like Scheme if I had the kind of life that went with butlers. I liked a lot of things about him, but most of all I liked the way he felt about his boss; I knew if someone ever pointed a gun at the Colonel, Scheme would step between them and take all six bullets, and he'd never consider falling before he'd caught every one of them.

Usually Scheme was more than ordinarily careful to keep a respectful distance, so I was surprised when he leaned close to me and whispered: "The Colonel's not what he was, Mr. Deco, since the operations. It would be extremely kind of you, sir, to make out as if he looked as he did in the old days."

It was just as well Scheme had given me that little warning since I might have widened my eyes or squinted them or otherwise shown I'd noticed something out of the norm.

"I find it helps considerably, sir," Scheme whispered, "to keep your eyes fixed on the photograph of the old gentleman!"

"I heard that, Scheme!"

A voice sounding remarkably like the Colonel's, considering it was apparently artificially produced, came from concealed speakers in all four walls.

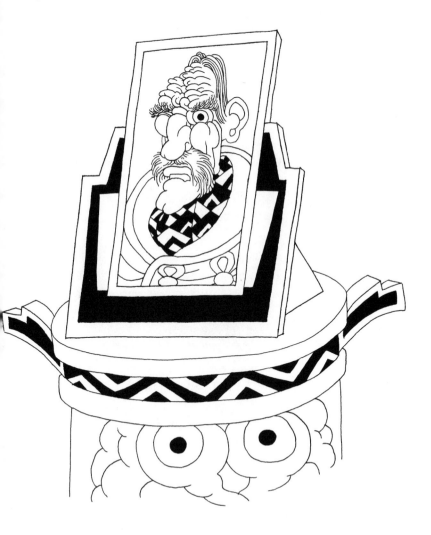

"Just don't tell me I'm looking good, Deco," the voice said. "Every damned fool who comes in here tells me that, and on top of everything else it's rather too much to bear!"

I nodded and gave a fair imitation of a smile as Scheme backed discreetly out of the room.

"It's nice to see you, again, Colonel," I said, "although I have to admit I'd expected to see more of you. Would you care for a drink? As I remember, we'd fallen into the habit of my making you one each time I fixed a fresh one for myself even back when you had hands, and I think I could use a little whiskey."

"A double bourbon, if you will, Deco. Neat, of course. If you simply pour it into the beaker it gives one something like the old effect. I've tried to get the doctors to work out some way of making this damned gadget smoke cigars, but of course they won't hear of it."

Maybe the doctors only left the Colonel his brain and eyes, but from the way he took in what I told him of his daughter's visit to my office, they still seemed to work as well as they did when he had the rest of himself wrapped around them.

"It's all gone sour from the moment she married that damned gangster McEstings, Deco. Everything else aside, gangsters are impossible socially. You've no idea how hard it is to hold dinner conversation with people of that nature."

"Yeah, I know," I said. "I've tried."

"Now some of his fellow villains have abducted the miserable creature and actually expect me to pay for his return," the Colonel's voice said, and I noticed little bubbles of what I figured to be anger rising from his brain in the beaker. "I would be willing to pay them to keep him, only I'm too well aware that people of that sort can't be relied upon to keep a bargain."

"So you sent Tracy to see me," I said.

"Excuse me a moment, Colonel," I said.

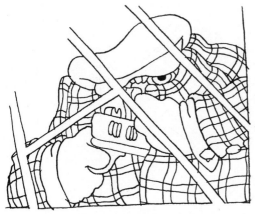

His shot missed the Colonel's beaker and my shot missed him, but that's the way it goes, sometimes. The two of us together had done a pretty good job of busting the window, which made it easier than it ordinarily would have been for me to jump through the frame.

I had to admit the old fellow was faster than he looked, but I was gaining on him easily and figured he'd be only feet away

when I dodged into an alley on his heels, but it turned out he was even closer than that.

Of course I would have known those big, flat feet anywhere, even without hearing the raspy voice that always goes with them.

"I think the gumshoe's finishing his little nap."

"Lieutenant Crowke," I said. "It's an honor to have your full attention. I can tell from your expression you're concerned, but don't worry, I'm fine, I'll live. You can tell your pal Rapper to stop smiling."

"You always could take a beating, Deco. I'll hand you that."

From the ground, I noticed, Crowke was very impressive, though I'll have to concede that from any point of view he is likely to put anybody with an ounce of brains on guard. First you notice how big he is, but you soon go on to realize that he's what you could call gnarled and that he seems to be covered in

tree bark instead of skin, and if you ever get hit by his fist, which I have on occasion, you're liable to get confused and think he did it with a club.

"A little old lady found you lying here in this alley," growled Crowke. "You've brightened her life, Deco. You've given her something she can talk about for weeks."

I pulled myself up by means of the dirty brick wall beside me because I didn't like having my face that close to Crowke's shoes, or Sergeant Rapper's either. Rapper's in particular, come to think of it.

"Did the lady see an old bum?" I asked them.

"Old bums taking you out these days, Deco?" Rapper asked.

"Let him go right now, Deco," Crowke said. "I mean before I'm finished asking you to do it."

I removed my hands from Rapper's greasy coat, brushing them off carefully in order to show how soiled they'd gotten from touching him, and then I grinned.

"I was just grabbing him to help myself up, Lieutenant," I said, speaking brightly the way somebody would if he was just trying to be helpful. "Like you might take hold of a garbage can."

Rapper and I have had a lot of little problems through the years, none of them resolved, and our little squabbles sometimes get on Crowke's nerves, but he brushed this one aside since he had more important matters on his mind. "The old bum's the guy who took a potshot at the Colonel?" he asked.

"Right," I said. "That and a weak lead concerning a Chinese laundryman named Wong Fat are all I've got to go on at this point if I'm to track down Lucky McEstings. I assume you know all about McEstings being kidnapped since you're otherwise so well informed."

Crowke took a cigarette out of his pocket, stuffed it into the usual corner of his mouth, and we all waited until he got the angle just right so that he could speak.

"I wouldn't count on getting much out of Wong Fat," he said. His talking made the cigarette wiggle like a little sword, and that brought it to his attention so he lit it, taking his own sweet time, of course.

"What do you mean by that?"

"I mean he's dead," said Crowke, using a combination of breath and smoke to say it. "I mean somebody sliced off the Chinaman's head for him."

"Chop-chop," said Rapper, enjoying himself because he liked the look on my face.

"When did this happen?" I asked.

"We were on the way from it when we heard about you decorating the floor of this alley," said Crowke, climbing into his car. He looked up at me just before he closed the door. "We've carted Wong Fat away, both parts of him, but I figure you'll want to look over what's left, so I'll tell the boys to let you snoop around, since you're a pretend detective."

He rolled up the window as the car pulled away, and I turned to head in the general direction of Chinatown, but the sidewalk was blocked.

"My employer, Mr. Gross, would like to offer you a ride in his limousine, sir, and to have a little chat."

I was surprised I hadn't noticed a car that large and black before, but then I had just been hit over the head and probably wasn't at my best.

"Tell your employer that his car reminds me too much of funerals and politicians," I said and made as if to go on my

way, but the sidewalk blocker took hold of my arm with one of his leather gauntlets and waved the opening in the end of the barrel of the automatic he was holding in the other just in case I hadn't noticed it, so after carefully weighing the various alternatives, I reluctantly accepted his master's invitation.

CHAPTER

◄ 3 ►

"I'm so glad we could get together, Mr. Deco, even though I deeply regret the element of threat that Hugo was forced to introduce due to your regrettable recalcitrance. Still, occasions shaped by impromptu measures are oftentimes the freshest and most pleasant we experience, now don't you find that so?"

The seat of the car was as large or larger than any I'd so far encountered, but Gross was fat enough to take up all of his side and a whole lot more of mine than I felt comfortable without. He and his fur coat put me in mind of large bears and walruses, the kind you're glad you're not sitting next to in the back of a limousine when you see them in their cages at the zoo.

"Please feel free to take anything you care to from the bar," he said. "Believe me when I say I want you to enjoy your ride as much as possible."

"Considering the circumstances," I said.

"Yes," he said, and chuckled. "Particularly considering the circumstances. I have some excellent champagne here, iced and ready in this silver bucket, though I expect that might not be to your taste."

"You guessed right," I said, reaching for something that looked a lot friendlier.

"No, Mr. Deco, not 'guessed.' I never guess when I can possibly avoid it, as guessing puts one in the hands of luck and luck is notoriously whimsical, don't you agree? The bar's well stocked, but more importantly I've laid in some O'Sullivan's Rye, which I understand is your particular favorite. It's what you've instinctively reached for and poured into your glass."

"It wasn't an instinct, it was a deduction."

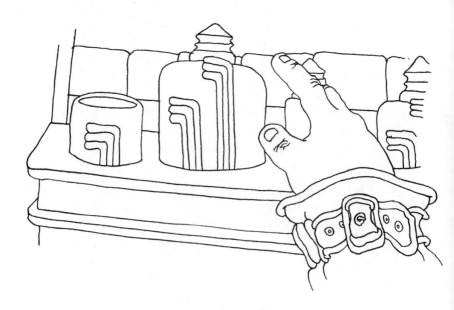

"I take it your pal in the driver's seat can shoot me through his little window any time he wants," I said.

"Good heavens, Mr. Deco, what a perfectly terrible notion—but I suppose he could; I suppose it's equally possible he might have other, even more unpleasant, alternatives available."

Gross leaned forward and I had a momentary feeling his flesh might break loose from his skeleton and engulf me like a mudslide. "Do you mind if I smoke a cigar? Would you care to? I have some fine Havanas!"

"I'm sorry, but I prefer cigarettes," I said. "I like the dry taste of the paper and the way it now and then sticks to your lips. I'm waiting for you to tell me why you've forced me into this hearse."

Gross chuckled again; he seemed to be fond of chuckling even if he really wasn't very good at it.

"I do enjoy the way you persist in returning to the point of things, Mr. Deco. I do indeed!"

"I don't want to overshoot Chinatown. Also it's possible if we became absorbed in idle conversation the time could fly by without our noticing it and we might find ourselves together in some remote and lonely spot."

Gross nodded and sucked his bulk more or less back onto his side of the seat.

"Then do, by all means, let us get to business.

"I am afraid that I and those I represent must most earnestly insist you restrict your investigations, Mr. Deco, to those sorts of problems you ordinarily unravel. We have no objection to your discovering murderers and locating stolen diamonds and all that kind of thing, no objection at all; indeed we've been amused, highly amused, by watching you at it through the years. We have nothing but the highest respect for your deductive abilities, sir, and for precisely that reason we are concerned that this case may present you with the seductive opportunity to push them further than you have ever previously done—to arrive, so to speak, at the other side of the solution. I feel it's only fair to warn you that there is a surprising profundity to your present puzzle, and that if you persist in digging into it you may find yourself unable to climb out of the hole produced."

"I like the nice way you say bad things to a person," I said. "You remind me of a shyster I kept having to deal with when I was with the department, but not having to cater to him or to people like him, such as the commissioner or the mayor, was one of my main reasons for leaving the cops and going it on my own, so you'll pardon me if I indulge myself by being occasionally thoughtless or rude, by not finishing your drink, for example."

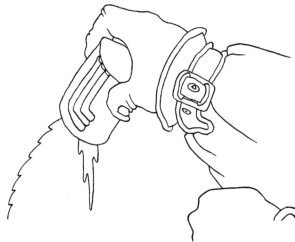

"You are very professional, sir. I must say I admire your sangfroid immensely."

"They teach it to all of us in detective school," I said. "Is there anything else you wanted to tell me before we finish? I see we've arrived at Wong Fat's."

"Nothing pressing, Mr. Deco. Hugo will let you out."

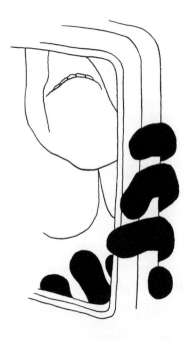

"Thanks for the lift," I said, breathing in the fresh air. "I'm not so sure about the little lecture."

"Remember it, sir. Mull it over."

I didn't like seeing Gross's hand being on the door while he was still sitting in his usual place way over to the other end of the seat, since that meant his arm was either a lot longer than

I had given him credit for or that he could stretch it like a squid, but I'd also noticed he was the sort of person who didn't seem to care which way his fingers bent, and I hadn't liked

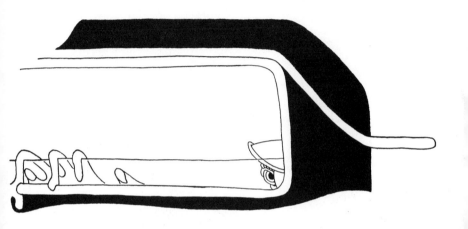

that, either, so maybe it was I just didn't like his type. Then he and Hugo and their big black car were gone and there I was standing in front of Wong Fat's place, surprised it was still a sunny day.

Crowke had been as good as his word and the cop on duty at the scene of the crime let me in like a doorman.

Since you're supposed to clean things in a laundry it struck me that the place could have used a little tidying up, but it seemed from the scarcity of packages on the shelves and their out-of-date tickets that cleaning clothes wasn't really the prime concern of Wong Fat's establishment, and that got me looking around to see if I could come across any signs of other activi-

ties, which was how I came to notice something odd above the left end of the second shelf.

I know it would be hard for the uninitiated to understand how Crowke and his men could miss first observing and then checking up on anything as peculiar as a laundry list growing out of a wall or even believe it would be possible, but anyone who's studied the work of the police department of this city for any length of time would tend not to be all that surprised or skeptical. I can remember one time when they spent a week stepping over a whole dead body without seeing it, but that's another story; maybe we can go into that some other time.

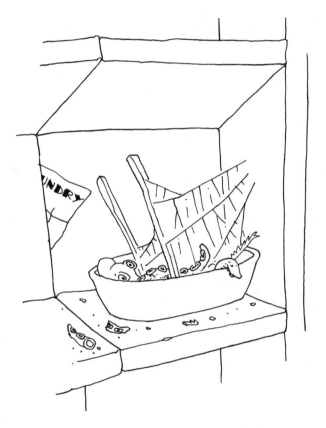

I did what you would have done, fooled around the walls looking for things that might move and turn out to be a catch or a handle, and it wasn't more than a couple of minutes before I figured out that if you gave a coat hook, which had no business being there in the first place, a twist to the right you found out Wong Fat's place wasn't a dead end in a whole lot of ways.

Deciding to go into that tunnel was one of those things you learn to do without too much thinking beforehand in my line of business, because if you go beyond the simple things, like checking to make sure your gun is really there and reminding yourself to keep your eyes open, you're liable to realize the risks you're taking and back out of the whole works.

Actually things weren't so bad since someone had been thoughtful enough to set an occasional kerosene lantern in a niche here and there so I could grope my way along without too much trouble, even if the place did wind around as if it had been built inside of a snake's gut.

It was narrow enough to start with, but it had been made even narrower because all along the walls on either side wicker boxes and wooden crates with Chinese stenciling had been piled to the rafters, and to make it look even more like a pirate's cave, here and there they'd tossed in bolts of silk, bright even in this dim light, and bundles of roots dried in weird tangles,

the kind old Chinamen simmer in pots in order to brew potions they hope will make them able to handle younger women.

This went on for some considerable time and then ended without warning in a smoky, low room with a beamed ceiling and lined with bunks like the passenger cabin in a slaver's clipper. The air had a thick smell with a caramel undertone that was sweet and bitter at the same time. I would have told you I could more or less see where I was going until I almost found myself stepping on something elegant and pale.

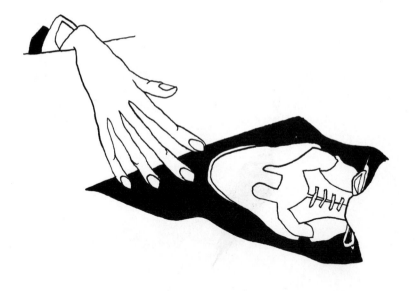

Frankly, the sight of a human hand on the floor of that place didn't surprise me all that much, but what I could make out of what it was attached to did strike me as odd enough to warrant picking up one of the lanterns for a closer look.

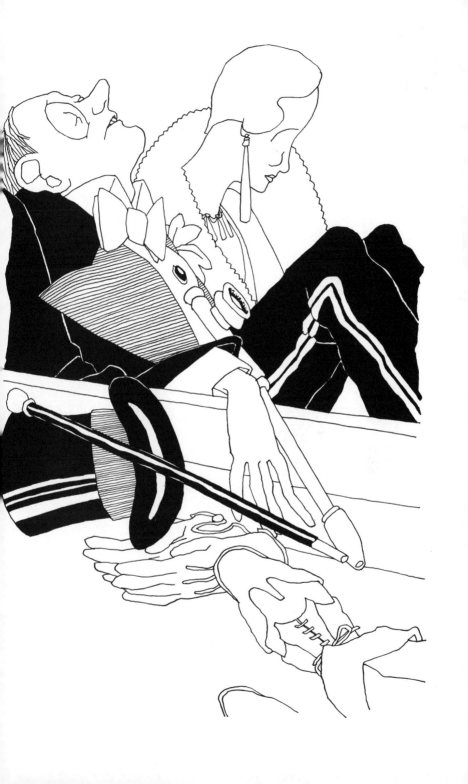

They weren't really the sort of people you'd expect to come across in a tunnel in back of a Chinese laundry,

but then opium addiction is nothing if not democratic, so any institution catering to the hobby has to be broad-minded.

I climbed a squat stairway at the other end of the room and opened the door at its head to find yet another tunnel, but this was worse than the one I'd just groped through because this one didn't put me in mind of pirates' caves; it reminded me of catacombs and crypts.

I decided to keep moving along since I knew there was nothing more than a perfectly ordinary laundry at the end I'd come from and had a fair idea there might be something more interesting than that up ahead. Then, coming around yet another bend, I heard two voices hissing at one another like a couple of snakes. The voices were speaking in Chinese, so the words weren't much help, but I didn't have to know the language to figure out it wasn't a nice conversation. I even figured out it might have something to do with me.

I crouched down behind a large black box I didn't like the look of in order to sort out what would be my next best move when somebody touched me on the shoulder and what hap-

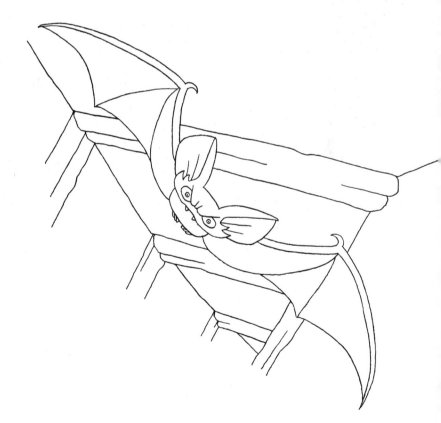

pened next was so quick and automatic it was as if I wasn't
doing it at all but only watching things happening to someone
else's body. I had my gun out and cocked and aimed and damn
near fired before I'd had a chance to look at her, but once I did
I realized that shooting her would have been a big mistake.

CHAPTER

◄ 4 ►

remember when I was a kid, one rainy day, I found a copper penny in the gutter; it was bright and shiny, like a little sun, and I couldn't believe my luck. I watch out for feelings like that, nowadays—I've learned to do so in my line of work —but seeing someone like her in a place like this put me in mind of that penny all the same.

Be that as it may, it struck me she was right about being on the quiet side, considering how close those voices were getting, and considering another, softer sound that I'd just now noticed coming from the opposite direction, so when she touched a certain part of the wall in back of her and it slid open a lot slicker than the secret panel in Wong Fat's laundry did I was impressed enough to follow her inside the thing, which put us at the mouth of yet another tunnel, and I even went further than that, I let her shut it on the two of us.

We'd only been standing there next to each other long enough for me to know she smelled like musk and teak, with something else I liked but couldn't identify curling around between, when I peered out through a cute little trick screen set into the panel, and what I saw made me glad I'd trusted her.

The old fellow back there in the bunk had been playing pos-

sum, and after he'd let me pass him by, he and his pals had formed two parts of a trap that would have sprung on me neat as you please if I'd still been somewhere out there between them.

They said a bunch of angry things among themselves while the old guy glared up and down the tunnel something fierce, and then they moved along, all three of them pretty clearly let down at not having gotten my head for a trophy.

"Thanks," I said. "I really appreciate it when someone saves my life."

But she'd put her finger over her lips again and now she led the way through a couple of turns, and then she did something to a wall and two new panels opened up, one behind her and another a little down the way. She stepped back into the opening behind her and lifted one of her small, strong hands to point at the panel behind me, and I saw it led to the outside. It was nice, after all these tunnels, to know there was still a world out there, but I turned back because what I really wanted to see was right here.

"Wait a minute," I said, speaking a little more quickly than I ordinarily do because her panel had begun to slide shut, "I don't even know your name."

She smiled.

"Looli," she said in exactly the voice I'd hoped she'd have. "Do you like it?"

"Let's talk about it over a drink," I said, but the panel had closed and she was gone. I stared at the wall until I realized that was a pretty stupid thing to do, and then I made my way to the panel she'd opened for me and stepped through it.

It was the first I'd known where I was in some while. The last time I'd been here was to bend over Bennie Souvestre and wonder who had put a line of neat little red holes going across the front of Bennie's boiled shirt and another line of big, ragged

ones, also red, coming out of his back and ruining his tux. My first thought then was that it probably had something to do with Rico, since he owned the club that backs up on the alley, and the way things had worked out it seemed I'd guessed right, but nothing ever came of it because Rico has an awful lot to say about what comes of things in this town.

Looking at a place like Rico's from the rear isn't playing fair; you're supposed to approach it from its façade because that way it looks as if it's going to be a lot of fun, and since I always like to do the right thing whenever possible I walked out of the alley and came into the place from the street.

The maître d's automatic smile faded when he recognized me, as I had now and then been a problem to him and his clientele in the past and had put some of his best tippers away for long terms in jail.

"I'll see if Mr. Spaldazzi's available," he said, and what he heard from the house phone on his pulpit made him lower his velvet rope and forced the grin back on his face. He didn't even have time to say he'd changed his mind about me before a huge man I knew loomed into sight behind him.

"Shoes," he said, "escort this gentleman to the Boss's office."

Shoes is maybe the largest thug of my acquaintance. We'd known each other for years but I had never so far shaken hands with him, not so much because I didn't like him—he wasn't a bad sort for the kind of guy who could beat you to death in an alley without giving it a second thought—but because he might forget to give my hand back.

"Hi there, Eddy," Shoes said.

"Hello, Shoes," I said, looking down.

"You like 'em, Eddy?" he asked.

"Altogether up to your standards, Shoes," I said.

"Take the usual precautions," snapped the maître d'. He didn't like Shoes chatting with me like an old friend; he wanted him to disfigure me.

"The Boss has been talking about you, Eddy," Shoes said as he went about his work, "but it's okay. I don't think it's because he wants to kill you."

"I'm glad to hear that, Shoes," I said. "I'm always glad to get through another day alive."

After the formalities of a little frisk were attended to, I was allowing myself to be led along to Rico's office when I heard something sweet and familiar that made me put my hand on Shoe's shoulder.

"Let's hold it here a little," I said. "I want to see an old friend."

"Babe," I said.

"Eddy."

If you were standing there watching the two of us I don't suppose you'd have to be a detective to know we'd been through a few things together. She still had that something in her eyes when she looked at me, and I guess I still had it in mine.

"How's it been going, old girl?" I asked.

"Can't complain."

"You never did."

Babe could sing a song up so you knew you were luckier than anybody else in the world just to be there listening to her do it, and she could sing a song down so you remembered all the things you wished you hadn't done, and knew you'd never get around to all those things you should do, but she was a lot more than that—she was the real stuff, regular any way you came at her, and I knew that better than most people.

"I didn't know you were here, kid," I said, "or I'd have come by before. Are you and Rico still an item?"

"He's a rat, Eddy, but he's my rat."

"You can't help who you fall for, Babe," I said. "We're all a bunch of suckers. I'm on my way to Rico's office now, or I'd have a couple with you and we'd talk about how it's going, but we'll do that soon another time."

"Another time, Eddy," Babe said.

Rico's office was as big as I remembered it, bigger maybe, but if you didn't know where to look, you might think it was empty. I knew where to look.

"Deco," he said.

"Rico."

He took a long pull at his cigar and gave me a look at his mean, squinty smile.

"We rhyme," he said. "You ever notice that?"

"Maybe we're two parts of the same poem," I said. I was hoping to wipe that smile from his face but it only got wider and nastier.

"You're cute, Deco; you've even been smart enough to give me a little trouble, now and then. I don't like you, I even hate your guts, but I got to say I'm glad you turned up because I've been trying to call you with a job offer, only my personal feelings kept getting in the way."

"I make it a point of pride to steer clear of your line of work, Rico."

"This is different. This is for what you do: for snooping, for sticking your schnozzola into other people's business. Have a cigar."

I passed on the cigar, but he'd gotten me curious enough to sit and watch as he spat it all out of his snap-turtle mouth like tiny bits of poison.

"For years, *years*, Deco, these guys have been trying to muscle in on me, see? Trying to get what was mine, this place, this property—actually trying to kick *me*, *Rico*, out of here! Can you believe it?"

He made his hands into rock-hard little fists and glared around his office.

"Say, they've pulled every trick there is! First they offered truckloads of dough, tried to buy the place; then they pulled some fancy legal stuff, tried to evict me; then came threats, and the next thing you know, people started getting killed! You know how it is."

"Yeah," I said, "it's tough, being a gangster. But who did all this, and why?"

"You think I ain't tried to find out? I put my best men on it, Deco, I gave it my personal attention, but no dice, no dice at all. And those we did kill and could get a good look at were strangers, out-of-town talent, dead bodies we couldn't track back."

He glared into space, probably looking at those bodies.

"And then, these last couple of weeks, something new, Deco —something I don't like at all."

"What's that, Rico?"

"Nothing!" He blinked, then shook his head. "Yeah, *nothing*, you heard it right, after a whole lot of something. After years of giving me trouble, Deco, years of not letting a week go by without trying some new trick, without ever letting up, they've just stopped cold."

He paused and ground out his cigar even though he'd only smoked it down a foot or so, and then his eyes focused on me.

"I've got a lead this time, and I want it followed up. Only I want it followed up good, see? not bollixed up the way these mugs I've got around here would do it. The boys spotted one of their people and nicked him but they didn't kill him—my orders—they let him crawl away and followed him so's he'd lead them back somewhere important, but he just holed up here."

I took the paper and studied it, but I must have looked pretty unenthusiastic because Rico said: "Listen, I'll pay you five times whatever you usually ask, Deco. Make that ten times. I don't want this screwed up, see? and I know you'll handle it better than anyone else in town. It's just for this once. And we're still enemies."

I nodded.

"Don't worry," I said, "I wouldn't have it any other way."

CHAPTER

I t would feel good to burn down all the Hotel Gilmans in this world and salt the earth they'd stood on, but then you'd just have to build them up again because there's an army of people who've lost the knack of living in any other kind of place. I like to think I'll never join that army, only in the middle of bad nights I sometimes wonder if maybe I won't end up enlisting after all, and it scares me.

I saw I could dispense with the usual formalities so far as the reception clerk was concerned, which put me around ten bucks to the good, and the spare key's being available cut the costs a little more.

The door to 304 looked the same as all the rest of them. It was painted in the same rotten copper green and the same

shaky hand had painted on its numbers, but I was careful to give it the full professional once-over, because if you don't people now and then kill you.

Scratches on and around its lock told about a lot of drunks, and a few bad repairs around its edges showed it was used to getting busted into, but that was all old news; the up-to-date stuff was the cluster of rusty brown spots on the floor along with a few thicker, wetter, bright red ones. Rico's boys had nicked this fellow pretty good. I pressed my ear carefully against the door's upper panel; there was someone in there, all right, and he was having a lot of problems breathing. I slipped the key in and opened the door as quickly and quietly as I could.

He tried for the gun when he saw me but only managed to knock it to the floor. I got hold of him with the idea of stopping him from making another grab at it, and ended up having a hard time helping him from falling out of his chair.

"You're in bad shape," I said.

"You don't look too good, yourself," he said. His voice wasn't much more than a weak whisper, but he still managed to get a pretty good snarl into it. "I suppose you've come here to finish me off, but if I was having a good day you wouldn't have a chance."

"I came here to ask you a few questions and then call for an ambulance," I said. "But now that I've seen you I may turn that around."

He blinked at me and shifted his head to a funny angle.

"You're not one of Rico's apes," he said, and blinked again. "You smell like a cop."

"I'd hoped I'd managed to wash that away," I said. "It was some time ago, and I've taken lots of showers since."

"It must have worked its way into your skin," he said. Then he sat up straight in his chair and grabbed my arm and I had to hand it to him, he had a hell of a grip for a dying man.

"I'm croaking, God damn it," he said. "I won't live to see it!"

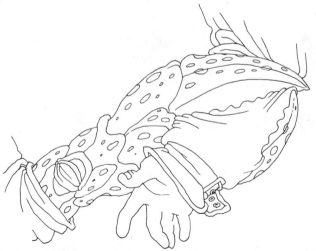

"See what?" I asked.

"I won't be there when we get away!" he said, and his grip got tight enough to really hurt, but when I bent to loosen it I got a big surprise, and I got another big surprise when I looked back at his head.

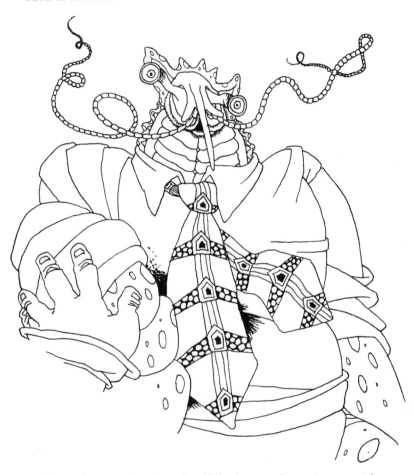

"I'm going to miss the takeoff!" whatever-he-or-it-was said. "God damn it! God damn it to hell! I ain't never going to leave this stinking place!"

It was getting a lot harder to keep him from falling because
he wasn't only getting heavier, his skin or his shell, or whatever
it was, was getting smooth and slippery under his clothes and I
couldn't manage a firm grip on the bastard anywhere.

"You know I'd really appreciate it a lot if you could explain
all this," I said. "And I think you'd better hurry."

"You wouldn't understand," he said. "None of you ever did
—that's how we got away with it!"

He gave a kind of laugh, one with not much fun in it, and
both because he was suddenly too heavy for me and because
he was no longer leaking blood but a kind of oily goo which

ruled out traction altogether, I lost my hold on him and he landed on the floor.

And then, just as it was dawning on me that I was lucky to have his body to prove all of this had actually happened,

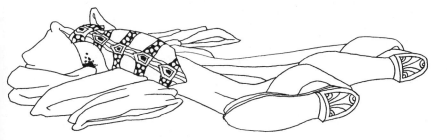

he melted.

"Where'd your friend go?" someone said.

"I was asking myself the same thing," I said. "But I see if you lose one friend, you gain another."

"You're a philosopher," he said. His voice was smooth and soft. He probably took it out and brushed it every morning.

"Just what I pick up in the popular magazines," I said.

"Maybe you could clear death up for me," he said. "I wonder about it sometimes, you know? Like, is it permanent? Is this heaven they talk about as classy as they make out or will it be a big letdown when you die? Would you like to be shot dead right here in this crummy hotel room and find out, or would you rather put up your hands while I relieve you of your gun? That sort of thing. I'm thinking all the time, you see."

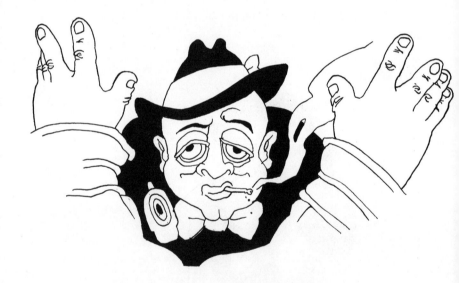

"Does this answer your questions?" I asked.

"Perfectly."

A lot of people in the wrong business think if they've got you to put your hands in the air they've made some sort of a deal with you which you'll stick by, and so they relax. My new little friend was one of them, so all I had to do was wait patiently and make it more than ordinarily difficult for him to remove my gun from its armpit holster—it's wonderful how hard it is if you don't lift your arm just so—until his mind drifted from his main job, which was to keep his full attention on my eyes.

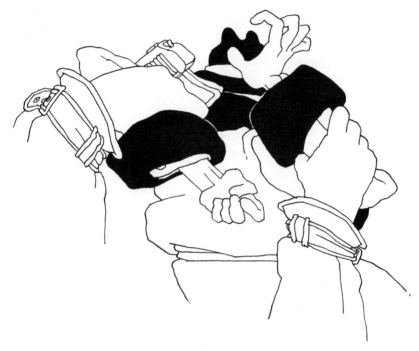

"Now I've got a philosophical question or two for you, pal, such as why were you paying a visit to the lobster? Be careful, the wrong answer could break your arm."

"You're hurting me, you know," he muttered.

"Actually, philosophically speaking, it's a good thing you showed up, since the seafood special had run out of answers. Maybe it's time for the next course, for the roast suckling pig. Maybe you can fill in the little gaps the crawfish left."

He didn't say anything, but he didn't have to. He was telling me plenty by the way he kept looking out of the window; not down and across the street at the low buildings squatting there, but high up and blocks away at the big, tall spoke of the Realm Building. I let my gaze slide along after his and it seemed to me I saw something glinting from the row of windows way up top at the base of its masthead.

"It's a pretty impressive structure, isn't it?" I asked him, keeping my tone conversational. "One of the prides of our city. You work there? You have friends there?"

He twisted against my grip as hard as he could, and that was a lot harder than I would have thought, but all it did was give me that warm glow I get in my gut when I know I'm on the right track. I upped the pressure on his arm and it didn't get a groan from him, but he did do some fancy wiggling.

"I hope you're not going to turn into an ugly animal like your buddy," I said. "I take away the pig idea; my guess is you're really an itty-bitty cockroach. That won't get you anywhere because cockroach legs break just as easy as arms, easier maybe, and there's more of them to break. You know I'm right about the Realm Building, now tell me about the lobster. Tell me about what he's going to miss because he's dead."

I had him down on one knee now, but the problem with threatening to break someone's arm is if he's smart enough and tough enough he can keep in mind that it's only an arm, so you might have to go ahead and break his other arm and then start thinking about his legs and then it gets involved. I know all that because I'm a philosopher.

But then he surprised me by suddenly spitting it out: "It's Wednesday! It's happening Wednesday!"

I didn't ease up because people are inclined to think you've got what you want if you ease up.

"What's happening Wednesday?"

"The getaway! We're busting out! We're making the big break!"

"Where's it taking place?" I asked, running through places people like to break out of, like Ming Ming prison upstate.

I've played it over in my head dozens of times, but I still haven't any idea how he got loose from me. Nobody'd busted that grip since Sergeant Mulrooney taught it to me way back in

police school. My only excuse is that he felt different, that he suddenly fit into my hands another way, so maybe he was changing into a cockroach after all—but if he was he got stopped because of another change, which was brought about when a bright beam of light came in the window and caught him just before he made the door.

I might have thought he'd done the vanishing act himself, since he was such a clever fellow, but the wall had done the same trick so it was pretty obvious someone else had done his vanishing for him in order to cut short our little chat. I might have hung around and made a few more clever deductions, but then I saw another glint coming from the top of the Realm Building and that convinced me I'd spent about as much time as I could in Room 304 of the Hotel Gilman and still live.

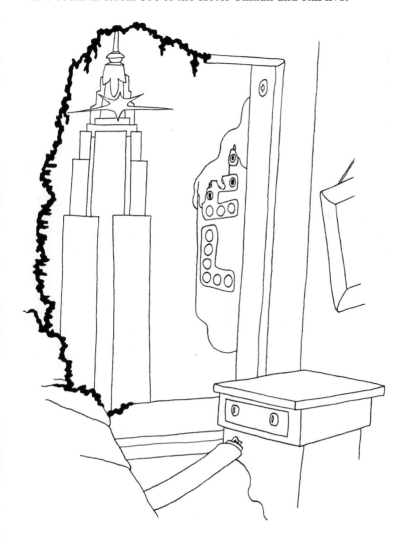

CHAPTER

I suppose expecting the hotel clerk to wake up and notice something had happened would have been too much to expect, and he hadn't, but I was a little surprised to see nobody in the street seemed to have noticed anything out of the ordinary, either.

Of course it takes a lot to get anybody's attention in this city; everybody seems to be willing to go pretty far out of their way not to notice things, and apparently burning a little hole in the side of the Hotel Gilman hadn't been enough to do it. Maybe it had been done too neatly and cleanly; maybe a cloud of smoke or a shower of sparks or, best of all, a loud explosion might have helped.

But then I noticed someone *had* been watching, after all.

I wasn't all that surprised when Gross and Esterhazy's daughter drove away very smoothly and quickly before I had a chance to ask if they'd liked the little show, so I took the trouble to light a cigarette instead, just to indicate their rudeness hadn't gotten me flustered.

I stood around and thought for a puff or two and then I headed for a little restaurant I know, not for the food—I tried that once and now I never go further than their coffee—but because of a friend and part-time employee I have hung out

there with more often than not; I figured he just might have the information I needed.

Taxi Charlie was there like I figured he would be. He doesn't make much of his living by hiring his hack—he uses it mostly to get him around town so he can keep up to date and you can usually find him at Tony's if you want to be kept up to date.

I figured Taxi Charlie might be particularly liable to have something for me since he parks his jitney in the big garage they've got under the Realm Building, and it turned out I was right.

He figured the best thing was to see for myself, so he threw in the ride for free and then he gave me a tour of the garage, which started with his getting us by the fellows at the door.

"Isn't going to the expense of hiring a couple as sweet as that overdoing it for a car park?" I asked Taxi Charlie.

"This is a very unusual place in lots of ways, Eddy," he said.

It was, indeed. For one thing, it was a lot bigger, and a lot deeper, than I'd guessed. "What goes up has to go down," was the way Taxi Charlie put it, and he told me he figured there has to be a kind of balance in skyscrapers: you can't be that tall without having a basement that turns out to be a good-sized building in itself, but he said even allowing for that he thought the Realm Building people had let themselves get carried away in the way of building basements.

I let him know I was impressed when we were standing on the seventh level with, at last, no further exit signs or ramps going down, but then he said: "I owe you for that time you stopped those guys from killing me that Christmas, Eddy, so I'm going to show you something." He waved me over to a solid-looking hunk of wall with a sign on it indicating we had come to the right place.

"For a long time I thought this was all there was to it," Taxi Charlie told me, "until I saw a trick a limo I'd been curious about pulled off. Every so often it'd come down here to the bottom to park, but nobody'd come up, and when I checked, there wouldn't be no sign of it. So I hid behind that pillar there and saw the driver do this little trick."

"What happened then?" I asked.

"This did," said Taxi Charlie.

PARKING FOR
MR. GROSS

Now I was even more impressed.

"I've never gone in there, Eddy," he said.

"And I don't think you should now, Charlie," I said. "This is my line of work. Thanks for this, and good-bye for now, and I'll tell you about how it all worked out after I survive."

So Taxi Charlie left and I started down. There were a lot of tubes and coils and all kinds of weird machines with lights on them together with a lot of other stuff I didn't recognize or begin to understand, but I knew none of it was what anybody figured had any business being here under the Realm Building, so it needed looking into and it was a good thing I was there since that was my specialty.

The main things in view were the ramp itself, which the oil stains and rubber tracks indicated got plenty of regular use,

and a funny kind of raised track on one side with a rubber belt, which was moving along a crazy mix of objects.

Ahead, or rather farther down, I could hear the steady pounding of large machines, and since it didn't sound far away maybe the real bottom of the Realm Building wasn't all that distant. I marched along a little farther but stopped in a crouch when I suddenly heard a flapping noise overhead.

I was on the ground with my gun out before I knew I'd done it, though it turned out I was in no danger as the flying thing paid me no mind at all; it just picked up a crate from the moving belt and flapped off. I stood and started on my way again and was beginning to think I'd almost reached the machinery from the sound of it when something about a long, transparent cylinder moving along on the ramp caught the corner of my eye. I walked over to take a closer look.

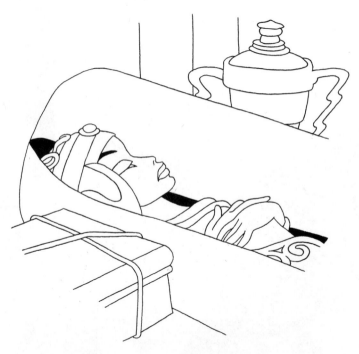

I wasn't able to stop the cylinder from moving along the belt and I couldn't spot any way to open the thing—there wasn't any seam or panel—so I began to pound at it, trying to break it with my fists, when I heard that flapping again and saw it was another one of those flying machines, only this one noticed me and noticed me plenty.

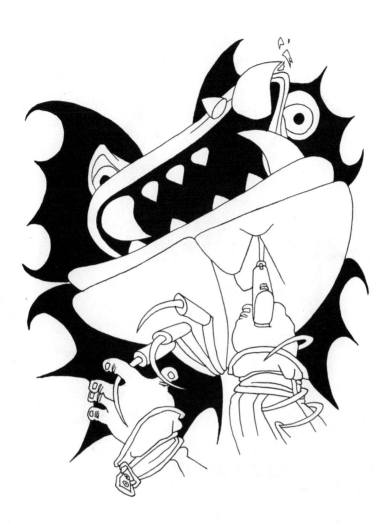

Both of us wanted that cylinder bad and we fought hard for it. The machine grabbed one part of it and I grabbed another and I got so wrapped up in wrestling for it I didn't realize the thing had flown the whole business of us into the air and was getting us higher every second. All along I'd been pumping bullets into the machine but with no effect whatever. I had just about decided it could eat as many bullets as I had to feed it when I suddenly got extremely desirable results just when I least expected it, which is very often the case in my kind of work.

After the cylinder fell and hit the ramp it finally broke but I just bounced. Looli tumbled out and I picked her up quickly and carefully because even if the flying machine was in pieces the pieces were still independently nasty, and I got one shoe scratched kicking aside the claws of one of its feet as they were scrambling over toward her legs and the other one seuffed when I landed a good one with my toe on a toothy chunk of its jaw that was heading for her neck.

Looli was limp and she was out, but her color was good and she seemed to be breathing regularly. At the first sight of her I'd dropped any thought of trying to find my way to the bottom of this place—my whole idea now was to get her out of here—but I hadn't gotten halfway back to the secret opening when down the ramp came something big and black and familiar and looking more like a hearse than ever.

Looli and I got a break because some kind of large gadget came by on the moving belt and I was able to get the two of us behind it so that for the moment Gross's driver couldn't get at us with his bullets, but all they had to do was back up to the opening with that limo and they'd have us plugged in here for as long as they wanted and could take care of us at their leisure. Even as I watched I could see that bright idea cross Hugo's thick face, or maybe Gross had whispered it to him from the back, and the car went into reverse and began to move and I figured that was probably it for Looli and for me, but it wasn't.

Taxi Charlie had come through, hack and all, and he gave Gross's limo a solid whack in its rear that almost knocked it sidewise while I rode past it on the belt, and then he slammed into reverse as I scrambled into the jitney's backseat with Looli. After that he got us out of there a lot quicker than I thought a taxicab could move.

One good thing about the bouncing around Taxi Charlie's fast driving gave the cab was that it woke Looli. I felt her stir in my arms, and then she looked up at me and smiled, just like we were old friends, and then she said: "I knew you would find me, Eddy Deco!" So everything was fine.

I waited until we were up a couple of levels and well out of there because I'm a little superstitious about calling in bets beforetimes, but when I figured we were all out of trouble, at least for then, I leaned forward and patted Taxi Charlie on the back.

"About that Christmas, Charlie," I said, "forget it. We are even."

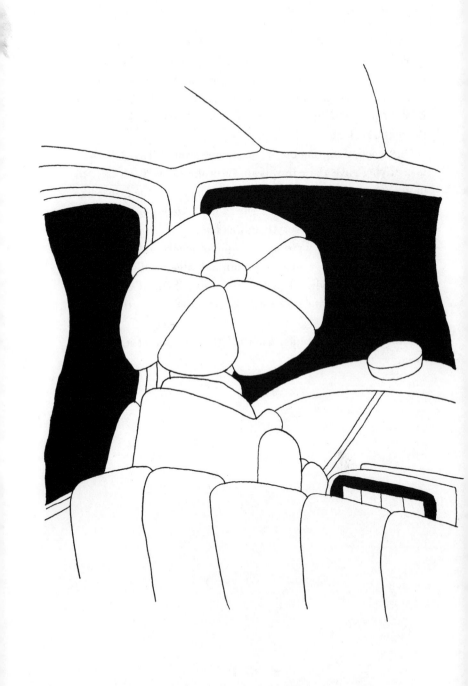

CHAPTER

◄ 7 ►

Being always strictly business, Taxi Charlie asked us: "Where to?"

"The Heron Building," Looli said. "The front entrance."

He nodded without slowing down, but then it was an easy target; you could see the aluminum trim on its spire from where we were. The Heron Building was the second tallest in the city, right after the Realm Building, so this was turning out to be a regular skyscraper tour.

"How did you come to be in that cylinder?" I asked Looli. "I take it you weren't there by choice."

"Your vanishing from Wong Fat's tunnels showed them there had to be another way out and they found it, and then they found me."

"I'm sorry I blew your hideaway," I said, and she smiled at me and surprised me by patting my hand. A girl I'd particularly liked in high school had patted my hand like that but nobody had done it since. I was glad it was being taken up again because I liked how it felt.

"It's all right," she said. "We were closing the whole place up, anyway. We were done with it. I had stayed behind after the others only to be sure we had not left anything of importance. The tunnels had to be cleared before Wednesday."

I sat up a little.

"You have plans for Wednesday, too?" I asked. "A fellow I just met started to tell me about Wednesday, only he got killed before he could finish."

"I'm very glad you got into this before Wednesday, Eddy Deco," she said. "Otherwise we might have left you behind."

"It must be some party you've all got planned," I said, but before she had time to go on about Wednesday the cab suddenly went around a corner on two wheels and took our minds off our conversation. I looked behind and saw Gross's limo taking its turn at seeing how fast it could tilt around the corner.

"I was pretty sure we'd have another dance with them," I said.

"People like that, you don't get rid of them the first try," said Taxi Charlie.

I wasn't all that worried since we'd done pretty well against that bunch up to now and looked to do even better now that we were on the open streets, but then I glanced to the rear again and the little hairs on the back of my neck stood up when I saw that a new and unexpected element had been introduced.

"Forget the Heron Building," I said. "It's too close, we'd never shake them. Head for Rico's Place."

"That might give us a chance to make them turn wrong a few times," Taxi Charlie agreed.

Taxi Charlie is more than ordinarily skillful when it comes to dodging pursuing cars. I know that for a fact as I've been with him when he's foiled experts—it'll be a while before I forget the sight of Ashcan Mantell driving his armored Nash off the Jefferson Bridge—but though your ordinary car can only follow after, and maybe spice things up with a meaningful fender bump from the rear and perhaps an occasional sideswipe, Gross's limo was actually trying to reach out and grab us.

"This is new," said Taxi Charlie. "This is definitely new. I have never before had to worry about long green things coming out of a pursuing car's windows, Eddy. This is a novel experience."

"They seem to be getting longer," I said. "If there's much less space between us they'll be able to put those funny suckers to work on your taxi and maybe on us, Charlie."

He didn't say anything in response to that but made his feelings about it pretty clear by means of increased speed and by making lots of funny little patterns in the streets, making sharp turns in unexpected directions around blocks chosen at random. All this served to increase my respect for Taxi Charlie's skill, but it made it very difficult for me to draw a bead on those tentacles curling out of the limo.

There were a lot more of them now, all of them still green, and since I figured there might be more to come, and since I didn't want that to happen, I leaned as far out of the window as

I could without actually leaving the car and concentrated on popping a few shots toward the cluster of tentacles on the left. I was in the process of observing that this didn't seem to produce any effect whatever when Taxi Charlie spoke up, loudly and firmly, with a high quavering note I had never heard in his voice before.

"Get it off me, Eddy," he said. "Get it off me quick!"

I pulled myself back into the car and pressed the gun into the shiny flesh of the thing where it bulged against the edge of the window and put three shots in a row in it, cutting it in two. The part inside began to fly around the cab's interior, bouncing off its walls and roof like a shrinking balloon, and the part outside shrunk like a curling watch spring back into the limo in the manner of a collapsing New Year's party squeaker.

"That is Kootook in that car," said Looli. "He is one of the Badgize."

"Yeah," I said, turning and squinting at her. "I didn't know about the first part, about his name, but I'd guessed he was one of the bad guys, all right. You know him?"

"We are deadly enemies," she said. "I hope someday you will kill him, Eddy Deco."

"I wouldn't be surprised if he doesn't force me to it," I said. "How's it going, Charlie?"

"I have a serious problem in that most of the wheels have been lifted from the pavement, Eddy. I dislike being rude to a fare, but I think you better leave. I think I better leave, too. Besides, there's Rico's, so we're here."

I fired a couple more shots into the tentacle that was trying to crawl through the door in a not particularly successful attempt to discourage it, pushed my way out while pulling Looli after me, and said: "You get her and yourself out of here and safely into Rico's, Charlie, and I'll do what I can to preoccupy our friend."

Taxi Charlie didn't ask any questions—it's one of his best qualities—he just grabbed Looli when I handed her over and began hauling her toward the entrance of Rico's Place. She didn't like it, but he was stronger and so he led her clear of the squirming and away—he was good dodging on his feet, too—which left me free to do what I could.

Even more tentacles seemed to have turned up in the meantime, but I was too busy just then to count how many as they were managing to get hold of a lot more of me than I wanted them to. In spite of my objecting as firmly as I knew how, which is with a lot of bullets, they were dragging me steadily closer to the limo when someone I'd seen before popped out of a doorway with a little present for Gross.

Up to now I wouldn't have been able to rake up a kind word

for the old bum in the plaid jacket, but I had to admit I liked the way he handled squids.

It seemed to take the heart out of all those green worms and they let me go so quick I fell backward onto the pavement, but

I scrambled up again just in time to dodge the limo, which was still running down the street at full tilt in spite of having become a great big bonfire. I watched it barrel past me and then careen flaming around the corner out of sight, and then I took off fast as I could after that monkey in the cap because I had a whole lot of questions left over from the time I'd chased him across town from Colonel Esterhazy's mansion and he'd knocked me out for my trouble.

He was still quick as ever and I figured we'd have a replay of
the whole thing except for that last part, but when a couple of
blocks of hard running led us into the fog of the waterfront
area, he made a sharp right into a little side street heading for
the docks, slid to a full stop in front of a gin mill, and then
sauntered in like he'd just been for a stroll.

I loaded my gun—it had been running out of bullets lately—put it in the pocket of my raincoat where my hand could rest comfortably on it, and followed him inside.

"This isn't much of a place," I said to the man in the cap, "but it's better than the dark alley I figured you and me would end up in."

"I was hoping you'd buy me a drink," he said. "God knows you've drunk plenty of my whiskey through the years, though you've been welcome to it, of course."

I'd been looking at him all along since you tend to keep your eye fixed pretty closely on someone who once went to the trouble of knocking you out, especially if you're wondering if he

might have another grenade on him, but now I let him come
into a different kind of focus and my mouth went a little dry.

"Damn it, Deco," and he said it with a sort of irritated bark
in his voice that he'd used on me plenty of times before when
he figured I hadn't come up to snuff, "I should have thought
you would have recognized me by now, even if I am wearing
this ghastly outfit."

"For Pete's sake," I said. It wasn't very clever, but then I didn't feel very clever for not recognizing him until just a short moment ago, and besides, it did a pretty good job of summing up how I felt. "Colonel Esterhazy. So you're not a brain in a fishbowl, after all."

"No," he said. "I'm a completely assembled human being who badly needs a drink."

I ordered us two large whiskeys,

we settled down with them in a booth while the Colonel brought me up to date, and it was quite a story.

Long before Lucky McEstings had married the Colonel's youngest daughter, my client with the veil, the old man had known Lucky was a crook, so when his brand-new son-in-law began to get himself involved in the family business the Colonel took the precaution of checking up on all his movements; this brought in a whole lot more information than he'd thought it would because McEstings had uncovered something about the Esterhazy real-estate ventures that none of his other employees had ever been dishonest enough to spot: it seemed a large number of supposedly unconnected investors who had signed leases back in the early 1900s on big chunks of his downtown property, and who had built some of the town's most important skyscrapers on them, had gone to an awful lot of trouble to cover up the fact that they were all part of one common group working together for some mysterious purpose that even McEstings hadn't figured out, for all his underground informants.

The Colonel admitted freely to being a man with a suspicious and grasping nature, it's a family trait, the one that's enabled the Esterhazys to acquire the rest of us lock, stock, and barrel over the generations, so he just naturally figured that anyone who had gone to all this trouble to pull the wool over his eyes, and who had succeeded, was not only involved in some scheme to get large chunks of his money, they had demonstrated they were maybe even smart enough to pull it off, providing he didn't personally attend to the matter, so he did a follow-up on the bunch, found out they had an office in the Realm Building, which was their major property, and stormed over there to give them a piece of his mind and find out what they were up to.

It surprised me when another bartender came up and asked us if we'd like a new drink; he didn't strike me as the type who went out of his way for the clientele, but I went along without

much of a struggle when the Colonel said he could use another, and we waited until it arrived and we'd had a few sips before he went on.

"I was even more suspicious when I saw them because of the strong impression they managed to give me that they'd done nothing wrong at all and that they were only too delighted at having this opportunity to get the whole thing cleared up; besides, their faces all had that look of frank, open honesty which is, to me, an almost sure indication of villainy. When they suggested we all retire to a building under construction where we might have a chat with a Mr. Gross, who would be more than happy to explain everything to me in detail, I went along with it because I realized I had up to now been dealing with underlings and that he might be someone whose arm was worth twisting. Of course I had no idea they were planning to murder me then and there."

"I think I'm getting to the point where I can start guessing the rest," I said. "Such as the first you knew they were actually trying to kill you was when they got you in the outside elevator, the one where the explosion took place. The explosion that was supposed to have turned you into an anatomical specimen floating in a jar."

"Just so, Deco. They waved me aboard the thing, then slammed its doors shut, and it was only when I found myself slowly going up the side of an unfinished building in an open cage containing a pile of boxes of dynamite with an infernal device ticking at their top that I finally realized I'd walked into a highly efficient death trap. Damn it, none of this would have happened if Tracy had had the sense to run off to Paris with a gigolo as her older sister did!"

"I read about the dynamite and all, me and everybody else. Only the papers told us it was an accident. And that brain they put in your mansion would have told me the same if I'd asked it. I made the mistake everybody made about that brain, Colonel, even Scheme. I thought it was you, so we didn't ask nearly as many questions about what happened as we should have."

I took another sip of the new drink and something my mouth and body had been trying to tell me for the last few minutes finally got through.

"So don't be too hard on yourself, Colonel, because we all make mistakes. Take us, for instance. Right now."

He looked at me and I wasn't surprised to see he was having problems focusing.

"I'm afraid I don't quite follow you, Deco," he said.

"We've just made a mistake, you and me," I said and raised my glass. "But, like I say, people make mistakes all the time, you see, and they shouldn't feel bad about it because it's only human. As a matter of fact it's often struck me that people spend far too much time brooding over their past mistakes. Excuse me if I wander.

"For example, we really shouldn't have had this second

drink, because it was doped, you see," I said, and it's possible I said a few more things to the Colonel, very likely something else about brooding, but I can't call any of it to mind because everything got covered with a big black wave just about then, in spite of my best efforts to push it away.

CHAPTER

I awoke with a headache that would ordinarily have gotten my full attention, but there were just too many distractions to allow me to concentrate on any one thing.

"You were certainly right about that second drink, Deco," I heard the Colonel say.

I turned—not without difficulty since I was tied by my wrists and ankles, spread-eagled on what I didn't need anybody to explain was a torture rack—toward the sound of his voice.

"I'd like to get my hands on the persons responsible for this!" he said. "It strikes me they're behaving intolerably!"

"I couldn't agree with you more, Colonel," I said. "Is there some way for you to unlatch that thing you're in? I'm trying to get at these ropes on my wrists, but so far it's not working. Try

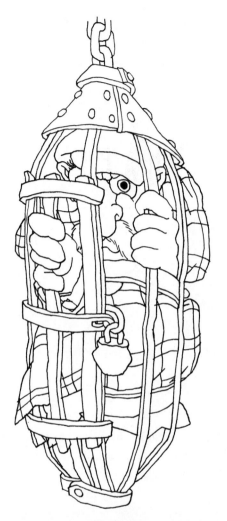

working the hinges on your cage door. It looks like the people running this torture chamber were bad housekeepers and let them turn rusty."

He set to twisting and wrenching the hinges.

"By George, you're right," he said. "I think they'll come apart!"

"By the way, and not to slow you down, how did you manage to get out of that elevator, anyway?"

"Only a moment or so before the explosion, the wire side of the cage next to the building began to glow and I saw that some kind of ray was being played on it. Aha!

"It won't be long, by gad, and I'll be free of this blasted contraption!" said the Colonel. "But to continue, the wall of the elevator simply vaporized, and that left me free to leap out onto the open floor we were passing and land behind a pile of scaffolding while the elevator continued going up one more story without me and then blew itself to smithereens."

"Did you happen to see which direction the ray was coming from? Did it come from the Realm Building?" I asked.

"It came from the opposite direction," he said, pulling the second hinge pin free and pushing open the door of his cage. "It came from the Heron Building."

"Just one last question, Colonel," I said. "Who or what is that thing in the jar passing itself off as your brain? And, by the way, my apologies for spoiling your aim."

"I can only tell you it is a most unwelcome guest in my house and that, someday, somehow, I look forward to taking another shot at it."

The Colonel made his way a little stiffly out of the cage, took a few unsteady steps when he landed on the floor, and then bumped into the iron maiden, which slowly swung open with a fingernails-on-the-blackboard kind of noise.

"Good heavens!" cried the Colonel. "Will you look at that! I must confess I never much liked the fellow, but in my worse moods I wouldn't have wished *that* on him! It's poor old Lucky McEstings, Deco!"

"Since I never met him before, I appreciate the formal introduction, Colonel," I said. "Now, if you'd come over here and untie me we can all settle down and have a little chat. I've been working at these ropes on my wrists, but I'm still trussed like a chicken."

He headed in my direction, but then there was a rattle of chains—this place didn't have any shortage of them—from the other side of the room. I turned to look, and found it was a little easier this time, which shows you how people can adapt to practically anything.

"You have another message from your boss, Hugo?" I asked. "Or is this just a social visit?"

"I came here to make absolutely sure you'd die, sir, as it was Mr. Gross's last wish."

"I'm glad to see you're not letting your formality down, Hugo," I told him. Then I said, "Seeing your chums here makes me wonder if I'm not back in Wong Fat's tunnels."

"A section of them you missed on your first tour, sir. These gentlemen are going to arrange this dynamite around you in order to blow you up. The Chinese have had a special talent for pyrotechnics since ancient times."

"Not more bloody dynamite!" said Colonel Esterhazy.

"I'd think you'd try something else," I said, "particularly in light of the Colonel's knack of avoiding the stuff's effect."

"That was not the fault of the dynamite, sir," said Hugo, "but of those who misused it. The Colonel will be a functioning part of the explosion this time around."

"Get to your proper work!" Hugo snapped, but before the old guy sulked off to help the others with the explosives, he managed to get in a sly, mean turn of the handle that showed me on the one hand that the people who'd built the rack had really known their stuff, but on the other hand, the right one, it showed that I'd done better than I thought at working on the ropes since it pulled that wrist loose, and to put the icing on the cake, it hadn't pulled it free enough for the others to notice.

"It isn't that I wouldn't have thoroughly enjoyed watching him at it, sir," said Hugo, smiling down at me, "it's just that we're awfully pressed for time."

"I wouldn't want you to miss Wednesday, Hugo," I said. "Too bad your boss, the fat octopus, won't make it."

"Actually, now I think of it, sir," he said, "it would seem a pity not to give you the benefit of a couple of good, bracing turns."

He started reaching for the handle of the rack like I hoped he would—maybe he could loosen the other wrist—but then I heard those chains again.

"Say," she said, "you really *are* sharp. You found my husband and everything!"

"Thank you," I said, smiling. "A satisfied client is our best advertisement."

She turned to Hugo.

"You haven't placed the dynamite," she said, and this time she didn't sound like Tracy McEstings at all.

"I'm sorry, madame, but Mr. Deco has been troublesome, and the Colonel—"

She gave him a slap out of nowhere that momentarily made his head change its angle.

"I don't care," she said. "They'll be dead in a few minutes if you'll just do your job. Stop madaming me and get to work."

But I had a little surprise for them because their argument had given me a chance to use my right hand and loosen my left hand.

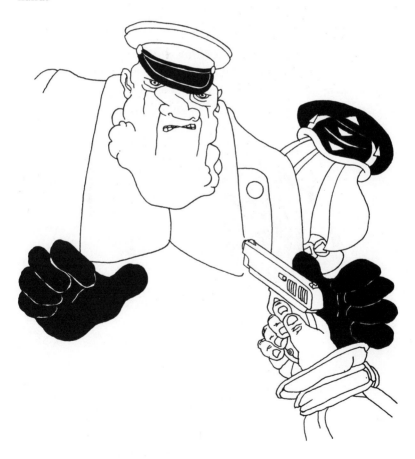

"All right, everybody," I said, "now we're all going to play a different game with brand-new rules. Colonel, you come over here and untie my ankles because I don't want to stop pointing my gun at these people for a second as they're very nasty and may try something, such as killing us right now without waiting for their dynamite to do the job for them."

"You should know something, Deco," Tracy said, in her new voice. "The timers on the explosives were set before these fools brought them here."

My feet were numb, but I could stand on them.

"That'll be your problem once we leave you with them," I said. "But before we do I want to satisfy my curiosity on one small point."

She started to back away at my approach, but I stopped her by pointing my gun at the biggest diamond on her necklace. I reached out and carefully took hold of a corner of her veil.

"I guess there's not very much point now in pretending to be Tracy anymore, now is there, Eddy?" she asked.

"No," I said, "I guess not. What did you do with her, anyway?"

"After we found she'd pulled you into this, we persuaded her to go to Paris. It was easy. Her sister will be furious."

"Stop right there," I said.

"You started it, Eddy," she said. "You wanted to see the real me, you gave me the old come-on. Say, kiddo, you weren't just teasing, were you?"

"I think we'd better get out of here, Deco," the Colonel said.

I began to answer but . . .

"Kill the Colonel, Hugo," she said, "while I dispose of Eddy here. I'm going to wind him up in webbing and turn him into a silly little sack of skin and bones."

I was just thinking about the funny tricks life can play on a guy, and the way you never know how it's all going to turn out, when all of a sudden events took a happier turn.

"Say," snarled Rico, and for the first time in my life I liked the sound of his voice, "you were right, Looli, kid—there's a lot of nasty bugs down here in the basement!"

CHAPTER

"Listen, let me tell you—I haven't had so much fun since we cornered the Mahoney gang in their Northside garage! What a swell turkey shoot!"

"I wouldn't be surprised if you haven't got the world record for spider legs, Rico, honey," said Babe.

"Yeah, I bet you cop that record what she says, boss," said Shoes. "I never seen such a big bug on two feet or how many it had!"

We were in Rico's place, us and nobody else, as he'd had it cleared of patrons, which is something you can do if you're a night-club owner and a despot. By the time Looli had sent Taxi Charlie off ahead with the Colonel to the Heron Building and cleaned and patched me up, he had a nice little champagne party going.

"I'm gonna have it stuffed and mounted on a big slab of mahogany polished to the nines with a shiny brass plaque saying how I killed it!" said Rico, but then he stopped and snapped his fingers. "Say, I could go get its head! Naw, I guess it's all blown up along with everything else down there. Pity. I can just see it over the fireplace, can't you, Deco?"

"Yeah, it would go great with the Christmas stockings," I said. "Look, I'm glad we're all happy on account of we're still alive, and this little celebration of it was just the break I needed, but Looli here just told me the Colonel and I slept a little longer than I guessed and that it's just turned Wednesday morning."

"So what?" asked Rico. "What's all this fuss about Wednesday? Why is everybody all the time going on and on about Wednesday?"

"Easy, Rico, sweetie," said Babe.

" 'Wednesday'! Wednesday'! God damn 'Wednesday'!"

"Wait a minute, Rico," I said.

"Wait a minute what?" he snarled.

"Don't you go telling the boss to wait a minute, Deco," said Shoes.

"Look at the shadow from your glass," I said. "The lamp's on your left side."

"So what?" asked Rico, blinking at me. "Who gives a damn?"

"The lamp was on your right side a minute ago," I said. "Did you move it? Did anybody else move it?"

"I didn't see nobody move it," said Shoes.

We all looked at the lamp. It stood there for a second or so, just as you would expect it to do; then it began, in a funny, sneaky kind of way, to creep back to Rico's right like a bad little lamp that had suddenly realized it had made a mistake in front of Mama and Papa and was trying to cover up.

"Boy," said Shoes, "gee, that's really something to see right in front of your eyes, ain't it, Rico?"

Rico growled and picked it up.

"I thought I'd seen everything working the clubs," said Babe, "but this one tops the list."

"Say, what is this, Shoes?" said Rico. "I didn't order any walking lamps with any lousy little legs on them! It's like to give the customers the heebie-jeebies, and they got enough heebie-jeebies to start! What the hell's going on?"

Rico hissed and jerked his hand away, leaving a smooth curve of bright red blood spots on the white table linen.

"It bit me!" he hollered. "The little bastard bit me!"

He grabbed the lamp again and then threw it on the floor. It landed on its side and bounced, but then righted itself neatly and ran off like a scared rabbit. It would have knocked over the champagne cooler, only . . .

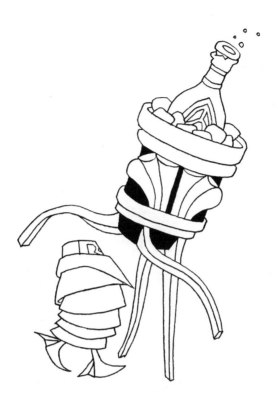

Rico cursed and sprang to his feet.

"Say, now it's the champagne cooler! Listen, I'm not going to put up with any more of this! This is all my stuff, see? I own everything and everyone around here, get me? I'm the boss! I won't have my junk running around anywhere it wants!"

Looli took my arm.

"It's the Badgize, Eddy," she said. "They're trying to ruin Wednesday, even if it spoils everything for all of us, even for themselves!"

"Don't worry, Looli," I said, patting her hand and trying to sound like I knew what I was talking about. "We'll give them better than they give us, kid."

I kept glancing around the tables cluttering Rico's nightclub because I couldn't shake the crawly idea that I was just missing seeing some important little movement out of the corner of my eye. Then, after a second or two, I spotted it.

It was the big, glittery, mirror-covered ball that hung over the dance floor. In the usual course of events it spun slowly on its axis and sent hundreds of separate beams of light over the room—that's what it did for a living—but now it was not only slowly spinning, it had left its usual place in the center of the

silver-starred ceiling and was gradually floating toward us like a small, nasty moon.

"Up there, Rico," I whispered. "Is that on purpose, does it do that all the time, or is that a surprise to you, too?"

"Say, now, this is really the limit!" he snapped, glaring up. "It's gotten like you can't trust *anything* to stay put around here!"

It was starting to slowly soar down, now; it seemed to be heading for a landing on our table, and the closer it got the more I had the feeling that each tiny mirror on its surface was a bright little eye.

"The bastard's *staring* at us!" said Rico—so he'd picked that up, too. "And it don't like us, and I know I don't like it!"

It was much brighter now. Somehow it had left off shining from reflected light and begun gleaming by itself. Then the gleam turned into a glare and the glare got so bright we had to either squint and shield our eyes with our hands or turn away.

I felt Looli's hand squeezing my arm and I heard Babe cry: "Stop it, Rico!" and suddenly both Rico and I had our guns out and were pumping bullets into it and the noise of our guns covered any noise it might have made as it exploded into a thousand pieces of light in every color I'd ever seen and a couple more besides. We were all blinded for a good minute, and when we'd blinked our way back into seeing, the nightclub stretching around us seemed as dim and dark as a cave.

"I'm sorry, Mr. Rico, but the Restaurant Workers Union don't like we should put up with these kind of conditions!"

"The union?" sneered Rico. "Are you kidding? I *am* the union, and don't you forget it!"

"Not tonight, you ain't, Mr. Rico, sir," said the maître d', and when he walked off, leaving his velvet rope and everything else behind, I saw he'd been the last to stick around.

"Say, how do you like that for gratitude?" said Rico, looking around at us for sympathy. "Everything's acting up, even the *people* I got around here. Anyways, maybe that's that!"

But I wasn't so sure it was because I'd just felt something hard and sharp-edged touch my ankle.

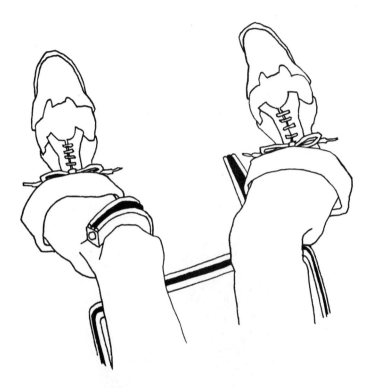

I stood and kicked the chair away and as it bounced back I saw all four of its legs squirming like snakes.

"Get back from the table and chairs!" I shouted. "Get clear of everything."

In no time at all we'd cleared a little space in the center of the club and were standing in a tight circle, back to back. I wasn't sure if I could actually see the tables around us moving, but you could hear the funny rustling the linen made, and the silverware and glasses tinkled like little kids snickering.

"I wish you lit this place brighter, Rico," I said.

"You're supposed to keep it dim like this," he said. "They say it's classier, and it don't show the dirt on the carpet."

"Hey, Rico," said Shoes. "There's something really funny about them wall lamps!"

"You're imagining things, you big ape!"
"Naw, Rico," he said. "Look again!"

"Yeah," said Rico, "I'm beginning to see what you mean, Shoes. We may have another problem here."

"I think we'd better leave, Eddy," said Looli. "It will be serious if I'm late."

"You seem to know an awful lot about what's going on here," said Rico. "What *is* going on here?"

"It is the Badgize," said Looli. "They have wanted your place for years. They wanted to build on it, but you fought them off—you have been very brave—and of course they hate you."

"Wait a minute," said Rico. "You mean those monkeys who've been trying all those real-estate tricks on me are doing this? Yeah, sure, it's sneaky, it's just their style. They *bugged* the joint. That spider in the basement was just a start!"

The wings on the things that used to be wall lamps all began to wave slightly, making a noise like a field full of snakes with metal rattles. It was as if listening to our conversation was getting them angry. A bunch of them were starting to move against the wall like bees in a hive; then one began to beat its wings and when they moved so quickly they became a shiny blue it detached itself from its holder and hovered in front of it like a hummingbird. Rico lifted his gun and fired at it and it flew apart like a cheap target in a carnival arcade.

"Say, they're not so much," he said.

"Yeah, boss," said Shoes, "but there's a lot of them."

"So what?" said Rico. "There's a lot of everything."

I took Looli's arm.

"I think she's right, Rico," I said. "I can see as how you want to stay here and fight it out—it's your ground, after all—but the lady's got to go and I've got to take her there, and that's the way it is."

I looked at Babe.

"You can come along if you want, Babe," I said. "It might be safer with us, it might not."

She smiled.

"I've got to stay with Rico, Eddy. He could get hurt. Rico needs me when he hurts, Eddy, you know that."

"Sure, kid," I said. "I know that. I just thought I'd make the offer. Take care of him. Take care of yourself."

Rico laughed because he'd just shot down another metal bat.

"They're not so tough," he said. Then he turned to Looli and me. "You two go ahead to wherever it is. Enjoy your Wednesday. I've got to stay and do a little housecleaning."

As if that were some kind of cue, every one of the shiny
metal bats broke loose of their holders and began a kind of
swarming, and at the same time all the lamps, still lit, hopped
off their tables and began running around on the floor. I remembered that the table lamps bit, and I figured the wall lamps
could do the same, if not a little worse, so it looked like we all
might be in trouble. Still, looking around at all that glittering
and sparkle, I had to admit the whole thing looked kind of
pretty.

CHAPTER

◄ 10 ►

We finally fought our way clear of Rico's, but it got pretty involved along toward the end because those flying lamps turned out to be swell little bullet dodgers once they got the hang of it, and plenty nastier than the standing ones so far as biting and scratching and inflicting other forms of damage were concerned, so before we managed to bust loose they'd cost me a few thin red lines across my face and a small part of my left earlobe, but since I'd thought to put my trench coat over Looli, she escaped none the worse for wear. She handed it back to me now and stared back at the dark outside of Rico's club as I slipped it on.

"Will they make it, Eddy?" she asked.

I gave it some thought because the last view I'd had of them they were in serious trouble. Shoes in particular had been so near to coated with flapping, buzzing lamps that about all you could make out of him clearly were his fancy brogans, but I'd noticed they'd been kicking, and kicking pretty good, so I told her: "I think it's better than even money they'll pull through, and my bet is that they do. They're a pretty tough bunch of cookies and it'll probably take more than a few lamps and tables and such to do them in. The important part is that they chose their stand and they're sticking with it."

The streets were dark now, but that's what you expect around two in the morning. What I didn't expect, and what we had, was that they were entirely empty except for a few stray newspapers blowing down gutters here and there, and that wasn't right at all, not in this part of town. I only saw one man, and him just barely, as he was ducking into a basement door. Everybody seemed to be hiding out, but from what?

Rico's was a long way from being the only night spot around the area, and the locals were famous for confusing midnight with noon. Ordinarily the clanging sound up ahead would have been buried in the noise of taxis gunning their engines and doormen blowing their whistles, but tonight it sounded loud and clear, even though someone or something seemed to try to muffle it at the end.

"What's that?" I asked.

Then, as if the noisemakers were trying to be helpful, I heard the same kind of sound, only this one came from about a half a block away in the other direction. I spun around just in time to see a black disk wobble and fall on the tar of the street in the light of a lamp on a nearby corner.

"That's a manhole cover," I said. "So I guess that's two manhole covers, and that makes it a trend. The question is, who's opening sewers this time of night? And why?"

Then a bright, flickering light came from both the openings,

and from several more of them I hadn't seen before, farther up and down the street. I saw a snaky stirring.

They were easy enough to make out since the sparks shooting from the sharp tips of their claws gave you more than enough light to see that if they got a grip on you you'd be toast.

"It looks like the city's high-power cables have taken a tip

on how to come to life from the stuff in Rico's joint," I said. "Those things are bad enough when they just flop around; I hate to think what they'll be able to do now they've started getting clever."

I didn't have to think about it at all as it turned out because the claw nearest to us snaked out and made a pretty good pass at grabbing the two of us on its first try. Luckily, and that was really all it was, it missed us and its fingers only made smoky little canyons in the sidewalk where we'd been before we leaped.

"My guess is we can make that alley ahead if we try real hard," I said, so we ran fast as we could, crouched down and as far from the curbs as possible, moving along the edge of the sidewalk that hugged the walls of the buildings.

Not that this stopped the claws from singeing us and stinging our faces with showers of sparks, but they did keep missing us by inches or parts of inches while they clawed trails of fire into the asphalt and churned the road into a stew, and I remember being particularly grateful when an overhead swipe that turned a Moxie poster into curly ribbons of charred paper and dripping tin just failed to scoop up the two of us before we made it into the alley.

Once we got well away from the road it took me at least a full minute before I got enough air back into my lungs to ask: "Is it going to be like this all over town?"

"One way or another," said Looli.

"So wherever we are in the city we're going to find streetcars turning into dragons and subways into giant worms. I take it these are the doings of your bad guys?"

"They're hoping it will stop us, or at least slow us down," she said. "That way they will have the advantage when noon comes and the truce is over."

One of the sewer claws made a grab for us and settled for a

few chunks of a building when it found we were out of reach, but I got a feeling it might find it had a little more cable to stretch with if it thought about it so the two of us backed up a little as it started bending a lamppost this way and that until it snapped with a pretty sparkle.

"You'll excuse my pointing it out," I said, "but it seems to me as if they're violating this truce of yours pretty good."

"They're a little insane," she said. "It's always been a great problem in dealing with them."

"I can see as how that would present a continuing challenge," I said, "but in the meantime everybody could get killed, hosts included."

"The sooner we go," said Looli, "the fewer will be hurt."

She looked up at me, and I could see it was a big look, an important one.

"My people must leave at noon, Eddy," she said, "all of us. Will you come with me?"

I studied her face and seriously considered asking her who she was and where we would be going and maybe even why, but then I thought the hell with it and threw the questions away.

"Yeah," I said. "Sure I'll come with you. Why not?"

She smiled and took hold of my hands and that took care of any doubts I might have had about its being the right decision.

"Only now you'll have to take something from me on faith," I said. "I promise I'll get you to the Heron Building on time, but we'll have to take a detour on the way. If the whole town has gone as nuts as Rico's place, and your word on it is that it has, I've got to check on Verna, to see if she's okay. Maybe things aren't what they were between us, but I guess that's probably mostly my fault. Besides, I owe her. There's a few bullets that might still be inside of me if it weren't for Verna, and a couple that never did get inside of me because of her, and one or two of them might have been the end of me."

Looli made no objection at all, so we headed for my office, and I can tell you it was quite a trip. We didn't run into any more of those cables, but there were plenty of other surprises along the way.

You've never been properly startled, for instance, if you haven't had a phone booth make a lunge for you with its folding doors without warning, and I can tell you from bitter experience that any time a fire escape crawls off the wall of its tenement and starts going for you, your best move is to let it have the whole block to itself, sidewalks and all.

Be that as it may, one way or another we eventually found ourselves standing across the street from the Rundown Building, and it was there that I saw the sight that has stayed with me longer and clearer than anything else I took in during that whole trek.

I think, ordinarily, I might not even have noticed the first of it, but recent events had gotten me into the habit of watching inanimate objects pretty closely, and I was in the process of giving the building's façade a detailed once-over when I picked up a faint motion over its entrance, a kind of faint flutter.

"She's trying her wings!" I said.

And as I watched she pushed herself up and then out and then she wasn't fixed to the front of the building anymore, she was hovering before it. I waved at her like a kid.

"That's good," I said. "That's something I'm glad I lived to see." And then I shouted: "Go for it, old girl!" and maybe she looked down at me, I'm not sure, and maybe she waved back, or it might be she was just reaching up, getting ready for her flight, and then her wings began to flap in a steady, strong rhythm, and she was free of it, free of the damned building I knew she'd hated all these years, and then she was up and going higher and all of a sudden the gold paint on her, which had gotten faded and patchy because nobody had looked after her, caught the sunlight and looked as new and bright as you could wish, and she went up, higher and higher, until she was a speck of light shining so bright against the sky it made your eyes water.

She was beautiful up there, just beautiful, and then she was gone.

CHAPTER

Since the lady over the door had been the only real decent thing the Rundown Building had ever had to offer, I wasn't all that optimistic about what we'd find she'd left behind. The place had been tricky enough before; who knew what it would be up to now that every fire hydrant and doorstop was seeing what it could do to get into trouble.

I noticed the door was just as filthy as ever. I rubbed a small spot of the door's glass free of grime in order to peek in, and when that didn't seem to help I pushed open the door and leaned in to peer around, saw that was more or less like sticking my head under polluted water, and finally admitted to myself we were going to have to step inside without any idea in particular of what would be waiting there.

The lobby had always been gloomy but now it was almost pitch dark because none of the dim little wall lamps were giving off their usual pale glow; as a matter of fact I couldn't even make out if they were there at all, so maybe they'd flown off like the ones at Rico's.

When my eyes adjusted a little I saw there'd been quite an impressive change in the wall at the rear of the lobby.

I'd never realized it before, but the sliding brass grillwork of the elevator doors had always been a comforting sight to me there where they belonged because they meant the elevator was snugly tucked away where it ought to be. Now I was looking at the empty shaft both because neither the doors nor the elevator itself were there to block it from view anymore, and because the opening had been violently enlarged, and that wasn't a comforting sight at all.

"It's loose," I said.

"What is?" asked Looli.

"The elevator," I said. "And it was bad enough when it was locked in its shaft."

We started up the steps heading for my office on the fourth floor, and everything went well enough until we got to the third-floor landing.

"I think those belong to our pal the elevator," I said. "It's not satisfied with avoiding giving us a lift—now it wants to block our way with its cables. That's got to mean it must be lurking somewhere nearby, so we may have a few problems getting up to my office."

"Or getting back," said Looli.

"Or getting back," I agreed.

We started stepping carefully over the thick, oily cables but froze when one of them shifted slightly.

"I didn't do that," I said. "Did you do that?"

"No," said Looli.

Then I heard a faint noise from the landing above.

"Eddy?" The voice was a lot thinner than usual but I had no trouble recognizing it.

"Verna? You up there, kid?"

I caught a faint gleam of bleached blond hair in the darkness overhead.

"Oh, Eddy," she said, "I was wondering where you were."

"I was on the case, Verna," I said, "but it got complicated, like they sometimes do, only this one more than most. Anyway, all that to one side, there's something I've got to tell you, kid."

"What's that, Eddy?"

"I've got to go somewhere, Verna, somewhere probably far away. The fact is I may be gone for quite some time, but I wanted to check and see how you were doing, what with the way things are, and make sure you were in one piece and all that."

"That was very nice of you, Eddy."

Then I heard a heavy, grating sound around the corner of the landing.

"It's the elevator, Eddy," Verna called down in a kind of a choked whisper. "I can see it from up here. It's working its way over toward you. It's been carrying on something terrible, Eddy, breaking up the walls and everything!"

"Yeah, I kind of guessed that might be what it was. Keep an eye on it for me," I said. "Anyhow, it's like I told you, I might be away for quite a stretch."

"How long?" asked Verna, and I glanced at Looli and Verna said, not so friendly this time, "Who's she?"

"Quite a while, Verna, it might even be a matter of years," I said, ignoring the business of who Looli might be. "I really couldn't say. You know how the detective business is."

There was a pause while Verna put all that together. I could always more or less tell from her face how her mind was working, I could do it even now, even in this bad light, so I knew when she'd worked her way through it before she spoke and could see she was pleased with where she'd got to with it.

"Well, it certainly is funny how sometimes things work out, isn't it, Eddy?" she said.

"What do you mean, Verna?"

"I mean it's really something," she said. "I was wondering how I was going to break it to you and how you'd take it and all, and now it's no problem."

"I don't think I'm following you, here, Verna," I said.

"I mean, now we can go ahead with our plans."

"Our plans?" I asked.

"Not your plans," she said. "*Our* plans."

"Whose plans?"

"Come on, Eddy," she said. "It isn't as if you couldn't guess."

Then I heard a kind of faint gurgling in the darkness up there beside her.

"You remember," said Verna.

"What?" I said.

"The thing," said Verna. "You remember."

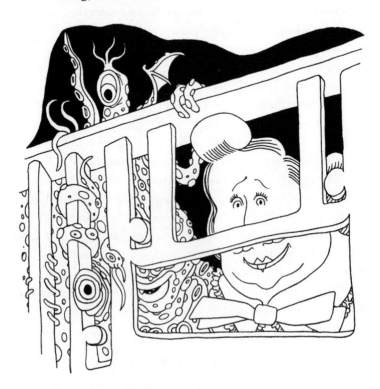

"Yeah, I remember," I said, "I've got a trained mind. It was waiting in the office at the start of all this."

"Well, we've done a lot of talking, the two of us," she said, "me and it. And we realized, just like that, we might start a detective agency on our own since I've had a lot of experience and it's very clever, and now I find out you're going to be gone for a long time—why, we can use your office, it'll be perfect!—so that's why I say it's really something how things work out. Isn't it?"

"It certainly is, Verna," I said, but then I heard that grating, crunching noise off to the side again.

"It's the elevator, Eddy," said Verna, and her voice had gone tiny again.

"Yeah," I said. "How close is it?"

"It's . . . "

"Never mind," I said. "Listen, Verna, it's all right, all of it, go right ahead and good luck, only now we've got to go, kid, so take care of yourself."

"Thanks, Eddy," she said. "You were always an okay guy. In spite of the other stuff.

"Keep in touch, Eddy!"

It was the last thing I ever heard Verna say and she shouted it because the elevator was suddenly swinging around, using its corner as a pivot, and you have to shout if you want to make yourself heard over an elevator scraping its bottom along a marble floor.

"It's got us, Eddy," Looli said. "It has us walled up in this little corner."

It seemed to, all right. There was maybe a little space, just a little, along the wall where we might sneak by, but it was mean enough to have left that tiny space on purpose so we'd try to sneak by and give it a chance to flatten us. It was quiet, now, except for the brass grille of its door, which it ground open and shut with a grasshopper's sidewise grinding motion; the lights inside its cabin glowed just a little, dimly, on the red side, something like the light that shines back at you from a hound's eyes.

"It's watching us, isn't it?" Looli asked.

"Yeah," I said, trying to be mad at Verna for not giving us enough warning, but not being able to make it stick because I knew our being trapped was my fault. "I'm going to try a trick, Looli; if it works, squeeze through that little space it's left us when I give the word."

I placed my shot as carefully as I could and when the red indicator lights that were mounted on either side of the cage door started blinking on and off with a regular rhythm I felt pretty proud of myself because I knew I'd been right on target and that the bullet had jammed the down button solid.

"What's going to happen now?" Looli asked.

"Watch," I said.

There was a pause, and then the elevator kind of gathered itself and made a sudden lurching motion.

"It's trying to crush us!" Looli said.

"It knows it can't," I said. "This corner we're trapped in works both ways."

The elevator lurched again, but this time it managed to lift itself a little higher since it had started to get the hang of how to do it better and you could make out the direction.

"Eddy," cried Looli, "it's trying to go down! It's trying to pound its way through the floor!"

"The old ways die hard," I said.

It made another jump, the best so far, getting parts of itself maybe as high as half a foot, but it couldn't really get itself entirely off the ground, of course, since it had deserted its vertical tracks, and some part of it always stayed on the floor; sometimes one corner, sometimes another. In the meantime, with all the terrific banging around, it kept shifting its position on the floor, which, by the way, it was starting to pulverize.

"It's not doing too well in the up-and-down business," I said, "but it's managed to jerk itself a little farther back from the wall, so let's make a break for it before the fool thing sees the error of its ways."

It was a little scary, sneaking past the thing as it heaved and crashed, sending up sprays of tiles and powdered cement and vibrating the I beams underpinning the landing, but we pushed aside the vision of what would happen to our feet, for instance, if it lurched our way. Looli got free and clear with no problems, but it cost me a wrist strap, a leather button, and a few black grease marks no cleaner would ever get out of the sleeve of my trench coat.

We headed down the steps two at a time, and I have to admit I was getting a little nervous because by now the whole stairway had started to shake and wiggle each time the elevator slammed back down onto its landing.

"From the racket it's making it must really be getting pretty good at pounding itself through that floor!" I shouted out as we rounded the last flight going down, and when we got to the lobby I looked up.

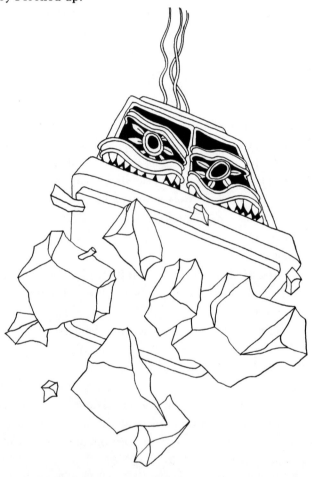

"Run, Looli!" I yelled out, "run fast as you can!"

And then, with a screech of steel on steel that made me grit my teeth and grin in pain, a combination of the elevator and the landing it had been pounding on came down as one whole business and landed with a bang and a roar that shook the building, and when the big white cloud of gritty dust had cleared, there was our metal friend squashed on the floor like a big brass beetle. It had taken its final trip down.

"It needs just one last touch," I said, "which I'll be more than happy to deliver."

And I was good as my word.

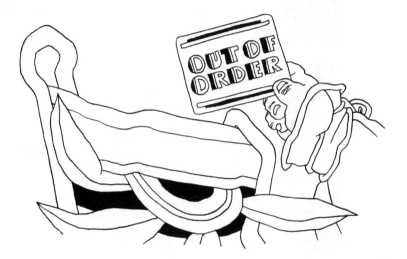

CHAPTER

◄ 12 ►

I might have been banged up a little more than I thought at the time because it does seem to me, now when I try to bring it all back, that I'm only able to remember what happened during the rest of our trip to the Heron Building in bits and patches, and the last part, just before we got there, isn't much more than a kind of a blur.

My brain still seemed to be working pretty well, though, and I can remember noticing as we made our way along that the bad guys seemed to have problems hatching the little tricks they liked to play on us in broad daylight, since all the attacks from now on came at us from shadowy corners or the insides of buildings, and that helped me figure out that they had to charge up what they used against us in dark, hidden places, away from the sun.

The flaps of mailboxes would lift, for instance, and letters would come fluttering out like big moths and try to smother us by covering our heads, or a dirty basement door would bang open and we'd have to dodge away from something clumsy, and clanking, patched together out of sooty tools, and once or twice packs of animals made up of bones and sour old rags came flapping at us from dusty bins in alleys.

But as I say, my recollections of most of these things are kind of fuzzy around the edges, though a couple of run-ins we had do stick out pretty clearly.

This came out of a number of garbage cans and put itself together at the same time it was chasing us down the block and gaining on us to boot. It actually looked bright and cheerful, you might say, all sparkle and shiny colors, but the first thing it did when it caught up with us was to show us how mean it could be with its sharp broken china fingernails and bits of mirror teeth.

I didn't have to spend many bullets to find out that my gun wasn't much use against it, since everything it was made up of had been broken already, and giving it a few more holes and cracks, or even knocking off sizable chunks along its edges, didn't even begin to slow it down. I have to confess I'm still a little proud of what I figured out in the end to do it in. I used a weapon against it that it could recognize and fear: I grabbed an empty garbage can from the sidewalk, turned it bottom side up, and clamped it over the thing like a candle snuffer. It worked like a charm.

Another problem we ran into that I remember pretty clearly came about as Looli and I were passing in front of a hardware store.

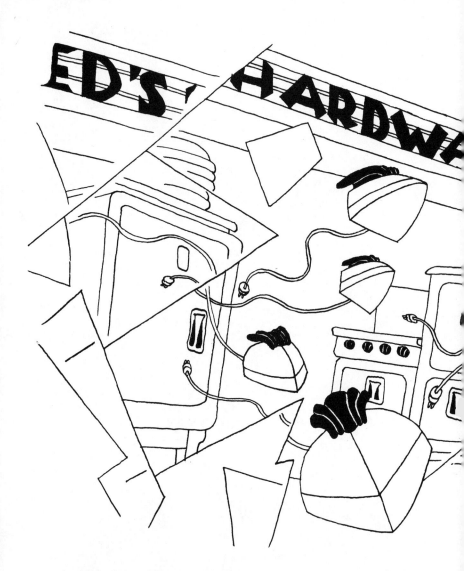

I'd often wondered why the people who design those sorts of things had taken to streamlining irons and coffeepots as I'd never seen the point of reducing the wind resistance on something that ordinarily only moved slowly from one part of a kitchen counter to another, and then with someone's help. They probably didn't have any good reason, those designers,

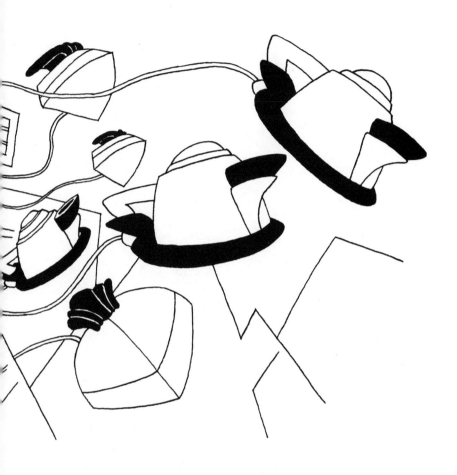

but I'll tell the world they handed those percolators and mixers a great big boost for that time when they went after Looli and me.

There wasn't a doubt in my mind at any point during the scrap we had with them that all those smooth surfaces and guiding airfoils were a great big help to them, and I can tell you from personal experience that their sharp frontal edges were very effective in attack, especially the irons'.

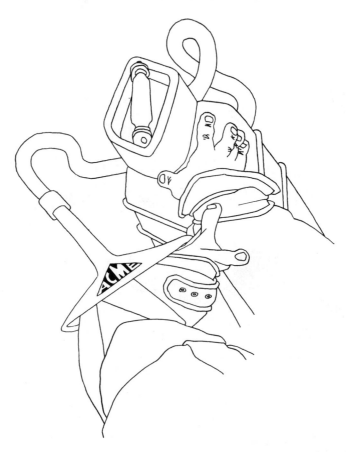

The first ones that got to me were what I came to think of as the snakes, and to this day I believe there was something more than a little personal about the way they tried to fight me to the death. All my life I'd never much liked vacuum cleaners, and it may be I'd now and then said unkind words about them in their hearing, as I'd lifted my feet in order to let one or another of them pass by; it's possible I'd complained about the awful racket they make once or twice while I was trying to talk over the telephone. Maybe they'd heard my thoughtless remarks and passed them on to their brothers and sisters, and that could explain why they seemed to go especially for me, to try to suck out my eyes in particular, and why none of them left off making the attempt until I'd torn their tubes apart, which, fortunately, I was able to do, and with considerable pleasure.

But each and every one of those appliances had worked out its own special technique, just as if they'd been brooding on their shelves all those years like a bunch of cons in stir and passed on to one another their schemes and plots on how they could each use some talent all their own to best get back at us for all that work they'd taken off our hands.

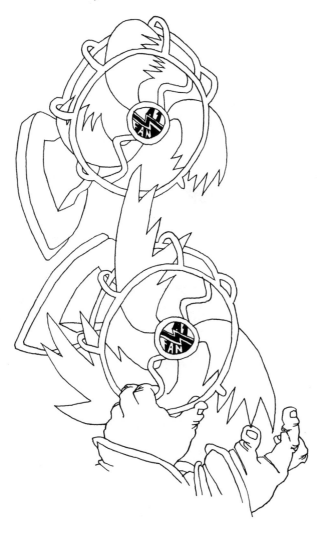

The fans, for example, had worked out the cute gimmick of cutting their power just when they were directly over you in order to drop smartly on the top of your head, and then—quickly, so it was difficult to grab them and smash them against a brick wall or a sidewalk—buzz back up into the air and drop on you again; the coffeepots had figured out how to soften you up with nasty little jets of steam before they started on you with their boiling water; the toasters in particular must have put a

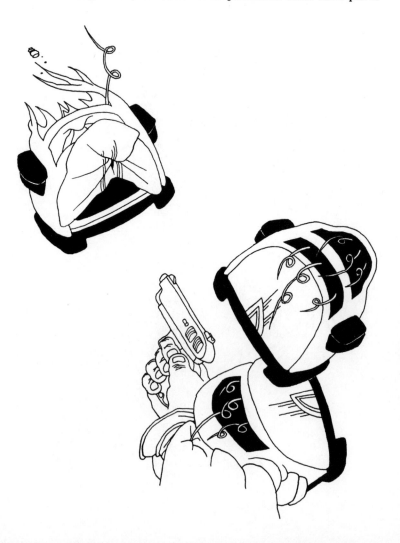

lot of thought into it because they'd figured out how to extend their heating coils, but they'd gotten too cute because if you could get by those red-hot little whips their trick had somehow made them fragile and easy to knock down; and the irons just kept coming at you, trying mostly for your head, but if you managed to get them with a bullet on their temperature dial it put them out of business.

I kept myself more or less hunched over Looli as much as I could, taking what I could of the punishment all that up-to-date household gear dished out, and as we kept moving along I was relieved to see that the sunlight and lack of darkness seemed to be getting to the things and that they were beginning to weaken and fall off, and after a little over five blocks all the appliances I hadn't managed to put out of order one way or another lost power on their own and they fell to the sidewalk one by one and lay there twitching and spinning, and I have to admit I was glad to see it happen, because if they'd kept at me just a little longer they might have managed to do me in and then they could have gotten past me to her.

But they hadn't, and now the Heron Building was just a little over a block off and getting closer, though it was slow work because I was having some trouble with my feet, but Looli's getting under my arm so I could lean on her made all the difference.

Being this near seemed to slow down the bad guys' doings, although a couple of windows half opened and a thing like a big paw slid part way over one of their sills and then stopped, and I heard something heavy trying to drag itself up the stairs of a subway kiosk, but nothing really got to us, nothing got close, and then, at the same time I could make out the brass buttons shining on the uniform of the doorman, I began to have a strong feeling I knew him well from somewhere else, and by the time

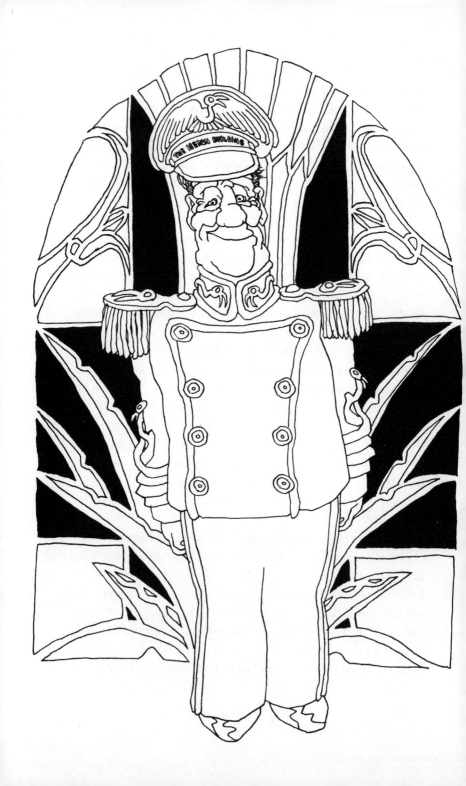

I'd dragged my way to the entrance with Looli's help, I'd made him.

"Scheme," I said, "why aren't you at the Colonel's?"

"It isn't the Colonel's anymore, sir. The Colonel is here, which is why I've just taken this job," said Scheme. "The Colonel's now belongs to that beastly thingummy in the jar pretenting to be the Colonel."

"So it does," I said. "I guess I'm not at my best."

"And no wonder, Mr. Deco, considering what you've gone through to bring the princess safely here. We all knew you wouldn't let the side down, Mr. Deco." Scheme said, and then he must have seen that whatever it was that had kept me going up to now was giving out because he reached over and took hold of my shoulders.

"She is a princess, isn't she, Scheme?" I said, and realized I was looking up at him because I'd slipped to the sidewalk in spite of his trying to stop me.

"So she is, sir," he said, and now he was kneeling down beside me without his doorman's coat because he'd taken it off and folded it with the brass buttons inside so it'd be soft when he put it under my head. "She is a princess, right enough."

And then I went out for the third time that case.

CHAPTER

·13·

I came to so quietly I had a couple of minutes to look around and locate myself and I was glad of that because I like to avoid having to ask where I am when I come to after one thing or another has temporarily put me out of the action.

I'd never been to the place, but I recognized it from pictures I'd seen in the Sunday sections in the papers and from postcards they have on display in racks where tourists hang out: it was the observation lounge on top of the Heron Building.

It was one of those spots I'd always more or less intended to get around to, and I was pleased to find it was altogether as classy as I'd been led to believe, but you usually don't find yourself going to the tops of tall buildings in this town if you're a local unless you're dragged up there by an aunt or an uncle

visiting the big city, and my aunts and uncles aren't the kind
that come to look up nephews.

"This is another time you've saved my life, Eddy."

"I'll always jump at the chance," I said.

I sat up, a little carefully, and looked around. There was a
small group of people up here with us; I didn't know any of

them except for the Colonel, who I saw over to one side peering down from a far window with a strange expression on his face. The rest of them were all bunched together over some kind of control board.

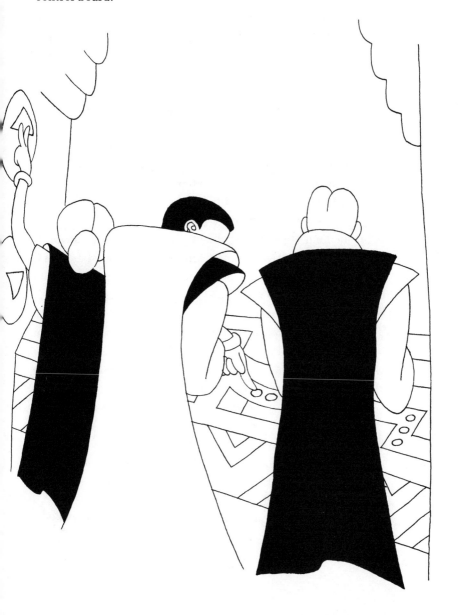

"Those may be tourists, Looli," I said, "but they're not from Kansas. And I've never come across a picture of the dingus they seem so fascinated with in any local guidebook."

"It was always concealed," said Looli, "and until today we all felt it was wiser to wear your native costumes."

I let that sink in, and then, since the sitting up had gone so well, I decided to take a whack at standing, but I'd no sooner gotten my feet on the floor than it seemed to tilt under them.

"Maybe I'm not doing so well at that," I said, grabbing at the window seat. Then I looked out and saw that the whole landscape of the city seemed to be tilting, so I elaborated on the theme a little: "No, I don't think I'm in good shape at all."

"It's all right," Looli said. "It's really happening. We're actually moving. The ship's gravitational device is still accumulating, but once it's achieved full strength you'll be able to walk on any surface you wish, like a fly."

I looked out at the city again. We were at the same angle. It wasn't the angle I was used to but at least it was the one I'd looked from before, only now I was looking from higher up because the Heron Building had risen like a concrete dirigible. But that wasn't the worst of it.

"I assume your bunch and those bad guys you're so steamed over are behind all of this," I said. "It looks like any building of any importance built since the twenties is taking off. You're even more impressive than I thought."

"Our technology is old and complex, Eddy," she said.

"I kind of knew all along you weren't homefolks," I said, and I automatically braced myself as the Heron Building tilted to a new angle as it began to follow along the east side of the city, but the gravity thingamajig was working just fine now and it didn't bother me a bit.

"Where is this thing headed, now that you've got it airborne?"

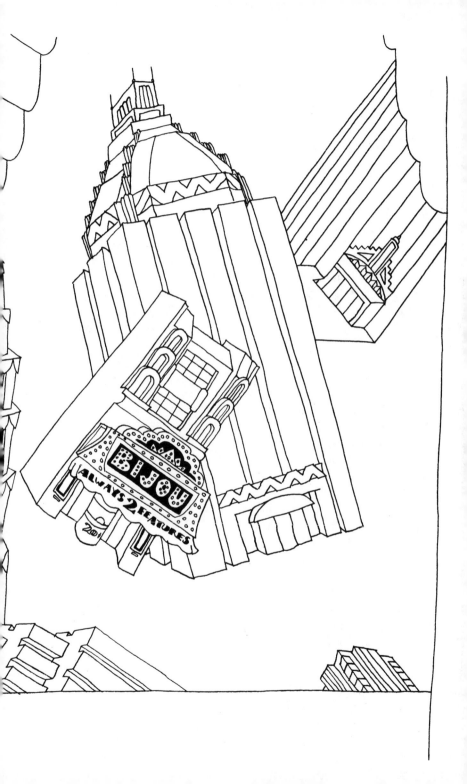

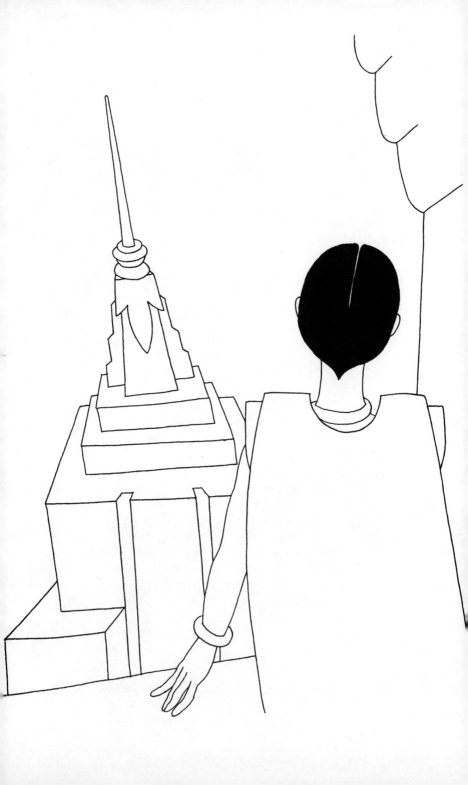

"To the Realm Building," said Looli, pointing. "This is our flagship, and that is theirs.

"My father and mother were the leaders of an expedition sent across the stars to pursue and destroy the remnants of the Badgize—stupid, evil beings who had nearly destroyed us all with their grasping, endless schemes for power. My parents' mission was to see to it that the creatures would never return to plague us again."

"It's coming clear to me why you held off on telling me all of this until now," I said. "I can see as how I might have found it a little hard to believe without a practical demonstration such as something like half the city's real estate taking to the air."

"My father paused to examine an astral object—your people call it Halley's Comet—and the Badgize took advantage of our scientific preoccupation by attacking us."

"It's difficult to keep ahead of people with one-track minds," I said.

"During the battle, in which my father was killed, our craft and the enemy's were hopelessly damaged and crashed together on Earth, which was then in the vicinity of the comet. After the crash my mother lived just long enough to give me birth. I was born here. I am an Earthling, Eddy."

We looked at each other for a moment, and then she went on.

"Since both ourselves and the Badgize were now marooned, we made a truce against the time when we could both construct enough new navies and continue the battle."

"So you both had the same problem: you had to put together a whole new fleet of spaceships without alarming the natives, such as myself, and you built them in disguise in full sight of the lot of us by inventing skyscrapers and all that goes with them."

"It was my mother's idea," said Looli. "We only merged our

ancient ethnic art forms with yours, which were, fortunately for ourselves, just then entering a period of extreme transition. That's why none of you noticed."

"And we thought we did it all by ourselves," I said.

Then I realized, by checking the view outside the window, that we were all standing upside down and it looked as if we were slowly but surely heading for a landing on the point of the building's spire, which didn't seem at all right to me even if I didn't know much about spaceships, and it looked as if the little bunch gathered about the machine I'd noticed earlier were even more concerned about it than I was.

We headed over there, as did the Colonel from his side of the room, and while Looli and her pals talked things over in a fluty language I knew I'd have trouble picking up, the Colonel and I chewed the problem over in English.

"I can't believe this is what they want the building to do, Deco," the Colonel said.

"I couldn't agree with you more, Colonel," I said, "although I guess we better get into the habit of calling it a ship. It seems unlikely they planned to stick it back into the ground right after they'd gone to so much trouble getting it to fly."

Then the whole bunch of us jumped at a sudden, wet, slapping sound against the main observation window.

"We may just have run into a particularly big bug," I said, "but I think all that goo may have something to do with your faulty steering."

We pressed close to the glass as more of the stuff squirmed onto it and other nearby windows, and I didn't like the way some of the larger panes were bowing in.

"All those things appear to lead off in the same direction," said the Colonel. "And, good heavens—look at what they're coming from!"

"It never fails," I said. "Just when I think one of those bad

guys of yours has turned into the ugliest thing I'll ever see,
another of them comes along and tops him."

"I know that thing!" the Colonel shouted. "By God I do!"

"I don't recall meeting it, offhand, myself," I said. "But maybe it was at a large party, or something like that, and it's just slipped my mind."

"You've met it, Deco," said the Colonel. "Or at least that part of it that's floating in its head, the only piece of it that's not translucent. Only it was smaller, then, and relatively helpless, and wearing my favorite smoking jacket to boot, so it's no wonder you have some trouble recognizing the thing—it's that damned brain that's been strutting around pretending to be me!"

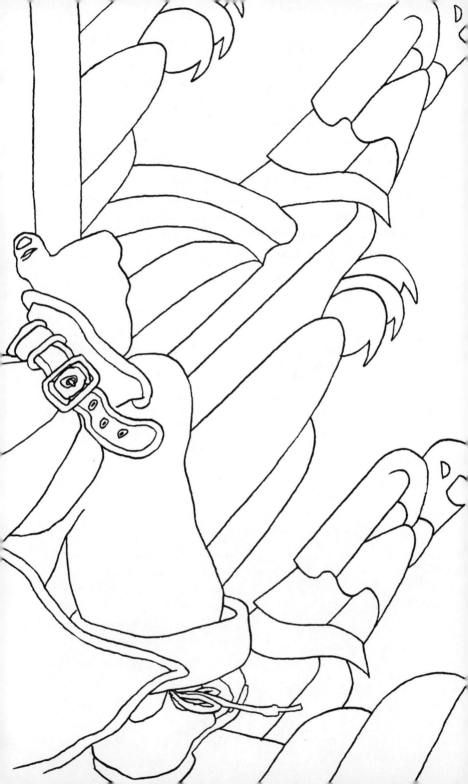

CHAPTER

◄ 14 ►

Since it was obvious that our staring at the thing was having no effect on it at all, I figured it might be a good idea if I made my way out there to see if I could do something positive about the situation, so I located a window I could open that was free of glop, and I crawled onto its sill.

That was okay, but then I found myself clinging to the frame for a second or two because there was an awful lot of empty space all around and a long fall down and a strong wind trying to blow off my hat, so just to make certain I was absolutely clear about a certain point, I leaned back into the window to ask Looli a question.

"Does this gravity dowhacky of yours work both outside and

inside, Princess? Am I right in assuming I can walk like a fly out here, too?"

"You can, Eddy," she said. "Only be a careful fly."

I let go of the frame then, and when I found that was no problem I put my feet over the sill and stood upright on the outside wall, which was now my floor. I gave a cocky little wave back at the folks staring out at me, felt my way for a couple of steps, and then I began walking, moving around the bright aluminum eagles that stuck out proudly from the building's sides and stepping over its shiny windows, and after a while the whole thing was as easy as strolling through the park.

I smiled and turned back and was thinking up something both flattering and clever to say about Looli's gravitational whatchamacallit when the smile got wiped off my face.

It was fat and squishy and altogether unpleasant and it was tugging hard, but I managed to pull my arm loose after a fairly tough little struggle. The thing had grabbed me with what seemed to be a kind of impromptu arm it had whipped together out of some sort of muscular jelly. I'd hardly finished getting myself pulled free of it when another glob of the stuff heaved up and flopped around my other arm, and I'd barely gotten done with working that one loose when I looked up and saw a whole new spread of the things oozing their way toward me over the windows and around the eagles.

I backed off respectfully, since I was pretty sure that if the thing got hold of me with those phony arms in more than two places with their whipped-together grippers I probably wouldn't be able to haul myself free. Then, just as an experiment, though I didn't have any high hopes, I snapped off a couple of shots at the stuff, and the results were about what I'd figured: the bullets just traveled in a foot or two and then settled down, comfy as truffles in aspic.

So that was a waste of time, and scrambling around the walls of the building trying to keep clear would be another, and time was just what the thing needed to succeed in crashing the whole kaboodle. I have to admit I was briefly at a loss, but when it reached out for a third try, eager as ever, it dawned on me that I might be able to get it into trouble if I just let it have its own way.

So I did.

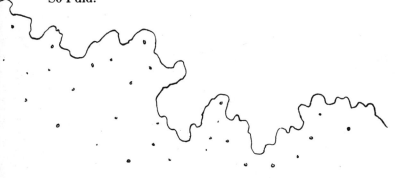

By the time I'd reloaded my gun and gotten comfortable, I'd been dragged halfway down the building and had a really good view of where I was going.

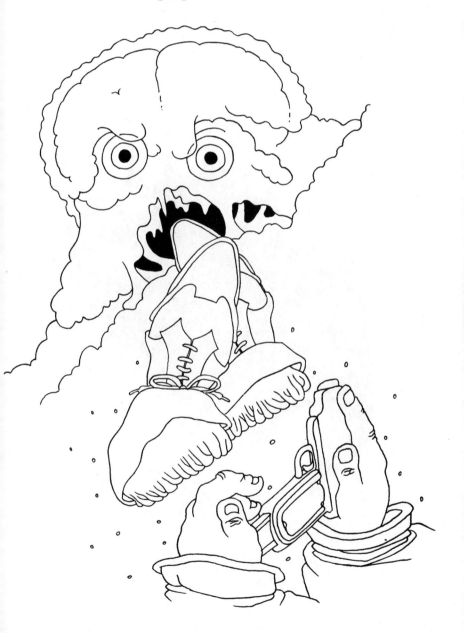

I looked back and could see Looli and the Colonel and some of the others leaning out of windows looking worried and shouting, so I smiled and waved to make them feel better, but it only seemed to confuse them. Meanwhile, the thing and I were really making progress.

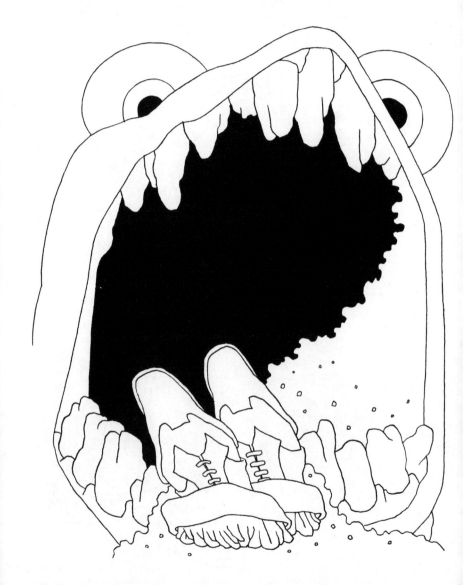

Everything was going along fine if my plan worked; otherwise I was just about to be eaten. However things worked out, it would all shortly be settled between us. It wasn't any time at all before I passed under the thing's soft palate, and of course that meant I was just about to proceed to its pharynx, or throat, to use the English, so it was now or never. I looked up and had to smile because there was my target, floating directly over my head. The thing had brought me right to it, as if by order.

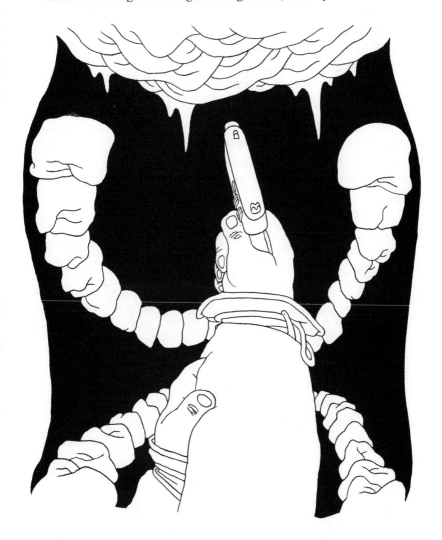

The Colonel had been dead right—it was the same brain I'd seen floating in the tank in his study, only now, by some bad-guy trick, it was puffed up like an ugly balloon. I had no idea if it had grown the huge jelly body it had around it now or put the thing on like a suit, but that didn't matter—the brain was its working core and that's what I was after.

I'd been holding my gun at the ready for just this moment, and now I pulled the trigger and kept pulling it until all it did was click. I'd guessed right: the brain was different from the jelly because bullets made holes in it that stayed there. Then, as I watched, some kind of gas came whinnying out of those holes, making their edges flutter, and the brain quivered and shrank.

The jelly of the thing's body began to cloud and fill with tiny bits of shiny green and I felt it grow stiff around me and for a heartbeat or two I wondered if I'd be sealed up and smothered in a huge leather mummy, but then I felt it crackle around me as I pushed against it, and then I stood and it crumbled into a pale green powder and I was free.

The powder turned into a fine dust and the wind blew it away. There were a few traces of it in the wrinkles of my trench coat, but they brushed away easily without even leaving any stain.

The brain was tiny, now, smaller even than I remembered it from the Colonel's study, and dry as a puffball. The wind caught it and it bounced along the wall of the building, catching a couple of times on the beaks and wing tips of the eagles, and then it blew off into the air and spiraled down and I lost sight of it in the wide, crazy-quilt spread of the city's streets and buildings below—so it seemed the gravity gadget didn't work too well on bad guys.

Then I noticed that I was looking at the city from right-side up and seeing it in less detail, which meant that the ship—now I thought of it as a ship—had pointed skyward again, so that

was all right; then I heard someone calling my name and turned and there was Looli, so that was all right, too.

"How did you like that?" I shouted.

"It was wonderful," she shouted back, "and so were you."

But then there was a bright flash, fierce enough to make me wince, and when I shook the tears out of my eyes I saw a gargoyle eagle next to me glisten and sag into a pool of melted metal.

A big shadow spread out over everything and I looked up to see the Realm Building, airborne now and moving slowly over us, big as a thousand whales.

I couldn't resist taking my gun out and reloading it and carefully firing every bullet into what would have been the building's heart region, even though I pretty much knew it didn't have one. I don't think it did much harm, that little gesture, but on the other hand it sure did me a lot of good.

There was another flash, brighter than the other because of the building's shadow, but this time it wasn't pointing almost exactly in my direction so I could see it as a ray coming from the Realm Building's top, and I'd already started running, moving faster than I'd ever moved in all my life, before it ended in a splash of hard light just short of Looli. I'd just scooped her up and was carrying her away in my arms from where the force of that second ray had knocked her when a third one hit on the side of the building where she'd been lying and all it left was a smooth, shiny round spot, so it was a good thing I hadn't stalled around.

Then we were back and Looli's people sort of poured out of the windows, and then the whole bunch of us all poured back together into the observation lounge, which had gone through quite a few fancy changes in my absence and was now definitely a no-kidding-around captain's bridge.

I stood Looli on the floor and she gave me a little hug and a look that I can still feel and then she turned and headed for all that jazzy equipment by the main window—the banks of dials and levers and so-on had spread out like a butterfly and went from wall to wall—and from the way she calmly started giving orders, and from the way they were obeyed, there wasn't a doubt in the world as to who was the captain on this captain's bridge.

CHAPTER

◄ 15 ►

"That was all very well done, Deco," the Colonel said. "You brought these people's general back to them like a proper hero!"

The two of us were standing a little to the rear since at this point neither one of us had too much to contribute. Looli was all business, leaning over the big control bank, looking out at the Realm Building, and listening to reports from her staff.

"I figured it was more or less my duty, Colonel," I said. "And she does look good there, doesn't she? Right at home."

But that's all either one of us had time to say because the battle had started in earnest now, and not just between our two big ships.

I had no idea how either side knew how to spot the enemy;

maybe everybody had programs, or maybe we were all willing to make a few mistakes. I couldn't tell the difference, myself, and I suppose that was why I could view the whole thing more impartially than I ordinarily would have been able to do and appreciate that, whatever else, it was far and away one of the prettiest fights I'd ever seen.

So far as we were concerned, it was a good thing the gravity dingus worked because Looli was really putting our ship through its paces as she dodged blasts from the Realm Building and jockeyed to throw back at least as good as she got, and usually better. The Realm Building was no slouch, either, but its larger size seemed to work against it, to slow it down, or maybe it was just that Loolie was the better pilot.

At this point in the battle neither one of us seemed to have any heavy edge on the other; we were like a couple of good, evenly matched boxers working each other over as hard as we could, but keeping an eye on the long run and watching our wind. We'd both given and received considerable punishment —I'd felt the whole ship leap under a couple of their hits—but we hadn't managed to get past the other's guard, and nothing vital had been hit hard enough on either side to make it really matter.

Looli's shots were good, though, and starting to tell. She kept reheating several big fiery patches she'd started until they began to glow steadily, and she'd managed to melt down a fairly important-looking section of the superstructure, and a series of holes she'd been drilling in a neat little row on the building's side irritated the bad guys so much they began a rolling turn, which was a little less smooth than their usual maneuvering in order to avoid her joining the holes up, and that brought its front square on to us, and from the buzz that went up from Looli and her bunch you knew that's just what they'd been trying to get them to do.

She reached out her hand and swept it across the buttons of the control board, playing it as you'd play an organ, and when that made the whole thing light up like a brand-new sign on a casino's opening night, she drew her arm back, shot a quick, sharp look at the target, and brought her fingertip down with a swoop to land spang in the middle of a big red button.

I think a kind of tremble ran through the whole ship—though I may have imagined it, I have to admit I was all stirred up—as more and more converging rays shot out until there were so many of them they formed a solid cone of light with its point burning into the middle of the upper third of the Realm Building, in the exact spot I'd aimed at earlier with my automatic.

"How about that?" I said. "So I was right about it's having a heart region, after all! Say, you know what you're doing or you don't, isn't that so, Colonel?"

The big building continued to move up—throughout the battle all the ships had continued to put more and more room between themselves and Earth—but now it began to move unevenly in a wavering sidewise spiral, all the time slowly pivoting on its own axis, and you knew it had the blind staggers, that it didn't want to do any of that. Then the layers of its fancy top towers began to sag in on themselves like a collapsing wedding cake, as if to remove any doubts from our minds that something serious had gone wrong.

"It's coming apart, by gad!" said the Colonel. "Look at those bits over there, floating off its sides!"

I saw them, too, funny little flapping flakes of all kinds of different sizes, and then I got a sort of chill and squinted my eyes to see if I could sharpen my focus because I wasn't at all sure the Colonel had read what he'd seen right, and it wasn't any time at all before I saw other things that made me doubt it even more.

The edges of the building seemed to have lost their ordinary sharpness, to have gone somehow fuzzy, and its walls had lost the clean, crisp look of steel and concrete and taken on a soft, blurred feel. Then I realized it was fair to say that the whole surface of the Realm Building was seething; worse than that, it was even fair to say that it was *crawling.*

I crossed the room to join Looli and by the time I'd reached

her side a couple of those little flapping bits the Colonel spotted
had come close enough to identify, so to speak.

"They're abandoning ship," Looli said, looking up at me,
"and now they're flying over to us."

"It's the bad guys' last and best transformation," I said.
"Their grand finale, and I'm impressed—they're changing into
anything they can think of that has wings. Do they want us to
take them aboard? Are they asking for help?"

"That would never cross their minds," said Looli.

And a moment later their leaders got close enough to show
how right she was.

"They're going to a lot of trouble to let us know that if we let
them in they'll kill us," I said. "Do you think any of them will
be able to bust through?"

"No," said Looli. "And at this altitude they're running out of
air. The larger ones can no longer fly, and soon none of them
will have enough to breathe. I told you the poor things were
mad."

"Say, will you look at all those stars behind them," I said.

"It's the universe, Eddy," said Looli. "We'll have a lot of fun up here."

"You bet we will," I said.

And we did, too.